Praise for Marianne K. Martin

"Under the Witness Tree is a multi-di
with rich themes of family and the sea
of discovery that reaches into the
beyond—into our community and its emerging history. Marianne
Martin achieves new heights with this lovingly researched and
intelligent novel."   Katherine V. Forrest

"Marianne Martin is a wonderful story teller and a graceful writer
with a light, witty touch with language and a sensitivity to the emotions of people in love. There is a tenderness and brightness to her
characterizations that make the personalities quite beguiling."
                                        Ann Bannon

"It is the interplay of personalities that makes Martin's novels a cut
above the usual lesbian love story."   *Mega Scene*

"*Mirrors* is a very fine novel, well worth your time and treasure."
                                        The Bay Area Reporter

"[*Legacy of Love*] is undoubtedly one of the finest . . . The sparring
between Bristo and Deanne alone makes it worth reading."
                                        Our Own Community Press

"Not only does [*Love in the Balance*] have love and excitement, but
it has issues very close to all of us."
                                        The Alabama Forum Gaiety

". . . wonderful language . . . [*Dawn of the Dance*] is a beautifully
written love story, filled with gentleness and drama."
                                        Mega Scene

If you would like more information about Marianne K. Martin and Bywaters Books please visit our website at www.bywaterbooks.com.

Under the Witness Tree

BY

MARIANNE K. MARTIN

Ann Arbor • New Orleans
2004

Printed in the United States of America on acid-free paper.

First Edition

Editors: Kelly Smith and J. M. Redmann
Cover designer: Bonnie Liss (Phoenix Graphics)

ISBN 1-932859-00-4

This novel is a work of fiction. Some actual people, places, and events have been used as historical fact to lend authenticity to the plot. All other characters and events are fictitious and are products of the author's imagination.

For Jo

Acknowledgments

Although writing is considered a solitary effort, no book ever reaches the bookshelves without the special contributions of many others. The author would like to take this opportunity to publicly acknowledge those contributions.

My humble thanks to the following people:

Therese Szymanski for her resources on the Civil War.

My sister, Trish, for giving me an understanding and appreciation for treasures of the past.

Jeanne Westby, reader extraordinaire, for her immeasurable encouragement and her honest, insightful input.

Jean Redmann for her much appreciated and valued editorial advice.

And Kelly Smith, whose support and encouragement is irreplaceable, for sharing her vision and her talent, and making me a better writer.

Secrets are only secrets as long as they remain untold. Some say the pain people suffer is in the keeping of them, knowing and playing God. Some say it's in the telling. And for some the pain is in suffering for someone else's secrets.

Chapter 1

Patience, calling upon patience. Dhari shifted her weight from her right foot to her left and resisted the urge to roll her eyes. *In Michigan I would have had my change, along with probably three other people, gone to the bathroom and checked my oil by this time. But this certainly isn't Michigan and the woman behind the counter is no doubt a nice woman with no clue of how my being plopped in the middle of this mess is disrupting my life. It's different here. Take a deep breath. It's only a few days. It can't be any more frustrating than dealing with Mom.*

The woman smiled, a cordial after-church smile, and fumbled with opening the end of a roll of quarters.

Just crack it open. Dhari shifted her weight again and tried not to look annoyed. "Smaller change is fine," she suggested.

"We always seem to run out of quarters first," the woman said. "I'll have them in just a second . . . see now that's what I get for bitin' my nails . . . there." She emptied the roll much too slowly into the drawer and counted out Dhari's change.

If change took this long, she hated to ask for directions. But what choice did she have? Get back in the car, try another place, and get the same slow response? No, she'd take her chances here. Dhari sighed and pulled a piece of paper from her pocket. "Can you give me directions to this place? Do I turn east or west from here?"

The blank look she received was one Dhari was quickly learning to interpret. She's not sure, but it's going to take her ten minutes to say so. "That's okay," Dhari offered, "I'll take my chances on east and see what happens."

"Springhill?" the woman asked. "The old Grayson place."

"Yes," Dhari replied gratefully.

"Lordy, it must be on past ten years since anyone's asked me about getting' out there. Miz Anna Grayson, she was some firecracker; Buddy, that's my daddy, 'member him telling me a story about her goin' after a rattlesnake with a shotgun. Like Buddy said, that snake didn't even stand a Custer's chance at Bull Run with that woman. So sad about her passin' away, but Lord she did live a life. Y'all related? I am sorry for your loss, I sure am. Oh, and that house, it sure was somethin'. I remember goin' out there when I was a kid for some big Fourth of July shindig. Boy I never seen such fireworks. She hired the entire Tolliver family, the men do the butcherin' and bar-b-quin', and you know how it is, the women do everything else. My Lord that was fun. Why that's when I first heard the story about Sherman burnin' a path right to the door of that house. Don't seem to be a natural reason it was spared. Not that I believe all those stories, mind you. You say you're relation?"

Dhari stopped jingling the keys impatiently in the pocket of her leather jacket. The woman was actually waiting for her response. "Yes, distant relation. A niece. I never knew her." Never heard her name mentioned once.

"Didn't think she had much family. Too bad you couldn't have come to visit before she passed on. I heard ole' Mrs. Tinker found her sittin' in her chair by the window. Fell asleep and never woke up. Guess that's the way I'd want to—"

"Yes, I suppose so." Dhari broke eye contact and motioned out the large glass window. "Did you say that was east or west that I should turn?"

"Oh, now listen to me ramblin' on. I nearly forgot to get you on your way." The woman stretched to the full extent of

2

her short frame to see up over the display in the window and pointed to the exit drive of the gas station. "You might-oughta take that drive right there and turn right, then right again on that road there, right there where that old sign stands. This here used to be Jimmy Holger's station; he and his brothers owned it for forty-some years. See the 'J' still hangin' up there on the sign? Oughta stay right on that drive. You'll be going west."

"Thank you," Dhari replied quickly, before the woman could take a breath. Finally. "Thank you very much."

Out there. The words were beginning to take on a whole new meaning. Once she had passed the sprawl of new housing communities on the northern outskirts of Atlanta, it was impossible not to appreciate the beauty of the Georgian countryside. Hillsides, sugarcoated with a light dusting of snow, glistened like a crystal forest in the first light of day. But the sun had since melted the beauty into miles of drab brown, leafless trees. The pavement turned to red clay and gravel, and houses with styles representing the decades, dotted the landscape.

Dhari reached blindly into her backpack and found the cell phone. She quickly dialed Jamie's number and waited through six rings. "Did I wake you?" The question was a formality. It was nine o'clock on a Saturday morning, of course she woke her.

"Sorry. I wanted to let you know that I got in okay . . . Yeah, it's not the RAV but it'll do for a couple of days . . . I don't know, I haven't seen it yet. I'm on my way out there now, but nobody warned me that I should've packed water and an extra day's rations. I'll call you later and let you know what I find . . . Why tomorrow . . . Do you have to go to the bar tonight?" Another question she already knew the answer to. Why do I ask? To see if I could be wrong just once? "Would you wait until next weekend? I'll get this thing wrapped up in a couple of days and I'll be back by then . . . I know they want to get together . . .

Yeah, okay, ask."

Believing that Jamie's friends would wait for her, though, was like believing in UFO's. Right out there on the edge of sanity. It wasn't going to happen and she knew it. They were Jamie's friends. In the three years that she had known them they had never gone out of their way to accommodate her; that's just the way things were.

It was no one's problem but her own, whether she trusted Jamie or not. Trusting her meant that her own angst was about being left out, about being of lesser importance, admittedly selfish. Not trusting was where things got tricky. It wasn't supposed to matter whether Jamie was a flirt, or merely an extraverted personality. Old friends and old lovers shouldn't be suspect. There had been no promises, no commitments. Exactly as Dhari wanted it. Paranoia wasn't supposed to happen. She crammed the phone back into the leather bag and pressed the accelerator harder.

"Where the hell is this place?"

Then she saw it, sitting far off the road on a graceful but neglected knoll. There, washed brilliant by the morning sunlight, stood the pride of Georgian architecture. Immediately, thoughts of a potentially high selling price and investments and a retirement fund raced through her mind.

She admired the sight all the way up the curving drive until the angle of the sun shifted and left the house in shadow. What had looked white in the sunlight was actually weathered clapboard and peeling paint. Apparent now from close range was a century of accumulated scars.

Old wooden shutters, some clinging stubbornly from one rusted hinge, offered a smile flawed by missing teeth. Once grand steps now sagged with age and neglected porch columns showed evidence of infestation.

With her hopes fading by the second, Dhari emerged from the car with a groan. Who in their right mind is going to want this? She started cautiously toward the side of the house following the remnants of an old plotted flower garden. Left now to compete against the weeds on their own, the dead remains

4

of liriope and rudbeckia share the once trimmed plots with thistle and chickweed.

She rounded the corner of the house where the sight of a tree, larger than any she had ever seen, stopped her in her tracks. What had seemed from the road to be a clump of tall trees was in fact one monumental tree. The width and breadth of it was nearly incomprehensible. Dhari looked above her as she walked beneath the canopy of its branches. City trees, planted in tiny plots of dirt between sidewalk and street, were merely twigs in comparison. Even without its leaves the tree created a shadowed world beneath it where only a few spears of sunlight reached the ground. Dhari shivered in the coolness. Only the giant sequoias, known to her only in pictures, Dhari imagined could best the magnificence of this tree.

She had nearly forgotten about the house. Maybe there was some hope. She continued to the edge of the shadows. Maybe I can sell it for the land, she thought. Her gaze wandered past an old trellis, covered with thorny vines, to what she could see of the property beyond the house. "The acreage alone has to be worth something," she muttered. I wonder how many acres . . .

"Been waitin' for ya."

Startled, Dhari whirled around to find an old woman sitting on a bench in the shadow of the huge tree. She caught her breath as the woman moved.

"You scared me," Dhari managed. "I didn't see you sitting there."

Although the old woman was standing now, she wasn't noticeably taller than when she was seated. "You believe in ghosts?" She asked moving forward and stopping short of the edge of the shadow.

Dhari recoiled a step. "No," she replied quickly. What the hell kind of question is that? Only a crazy woman would ask such a thing.

"Mm, no matter," she said as she closed the distance between them.

Dhari watched the tiny woman emerge into the sunlight. Black pearls looked with intensity from the raisin-like face. Just a harmless old woman, that's all. Dhari took a more normal breath. "Do you live nearby?"

"Raised up right here on dis lan. Never saw no need to go nowhere else."

Right here? She hadn't quite decided whether to question further when the old woman obliged her.

"My family's been here long as yorn, workin' da lan before we was free, workin' it after. Nessie Tinker, dat's me."

"You're the one who found my aunt." The old woman made no acknowledgement. "After she died."

"Miz Anna jus lef dem ol' tired bones. She don't ache no more."

Dhari nodded. The uneasiness she felt under the old woman's stare was still there. What is her concern with me, especially now? What does she want?

"I think I'll take a look inside."

"All ready for ya. Fresh fixins in da kitchen. Clean bed sheets."

"Oh . . . well, thank you. That was very nice of you, but I hadn't planned on staying. I'll only be here a few days. I got a motel room near the highway." Dhari looked back at the house and noted a back door. "Where is it you said you lived?"

Nessie motioned toward a well-traveled path leading through the tall grass at the rear of the house. "Jus over dere."

The roof of a small one-story building was visible over the crest of a sloping hill. More than a healthy walk for such an old woman, Dhari thought, before movement at the start of the path caught her attention. Nessie, with remarkable swiftness, was on her way home.

"Nessie," Dhari called, "thank you for preparing things for me."

Nessie nodded and held up the back of her hand and disappeared around a turn of tall grass.

I wonder how many trips it takes to keep a path so worn. What kind of person was Anna Grayson to keep a woman that old working for a wage? Selfishness? Loyalty? And how will she survive now? Maybe I wouldn't have wanted to know Anna Grayson at all.

She watched for a moment without seeing even so much as the top of Nessie's head moving along the path, then continued into the house. The inside was as she had expected, full of old furniture, creaky floors covered by worn rugs, and looking as it had, probably, for most of her aunt's life. It was, however, cleaner and neater than she had imagined. Actually, immaculate would be a fairer description, a pleasant contrast to the exterior. At least the furnishings, in their pristine condition, would bring a fair price from antique dealers and collectors. She made a mental note to ask for a reputable name from the realtor. Now to find a realtor that I can trust to handle everything by phone.

Chapter 2

Thankfully the Atlanta area offered a wide choice of gay, gay-friendly, and women realtors. Dhari filtered through a variety of responses that all basically said "can't get to you until next week," and settled on a woman whose phone voice resonated like a slow-moving freight train—steady, methodical, and reassuring. It was a sound she could trust, she decided, and one she wouldn't mind hearing on the other end of the phone for as long as it took.

Face to face, Terri Sandler was taller than Dhari had imagined, with football league shoulders and the weight of a lineman. The initial intimidation, however, vanished immediately with her warm handshake and illuminating smile. Dhari relaxed instantly and settled into the chair facing the desk, wondering if she looked as small and feminine to Terri Sandler as she felt right now.

"You mentioned that your flight leaves on Wednesday, but you didn't say where home is."

"Canton, Michigan, just outside of Detroit. Suburbia," Dhari smiled. "Outside the congestion and annoyances of a big city, yet close enough to get to whatever's happening."

"Exactly why I chose Marietta and an office in this little mall." Terri leaned back and pulled a paper from the fax machine behind her. "I got what information was available from the register's office on the property." She looked over the sheet quickly before continuing. "When were you planning on coming back?"

Dhari raised her eyebrows and offered a slight shrug. "If I really have to I suppose I could get back in a couple of weeks. I still have to hook up with someone who can handle an auction or estate sale for me. I was hoping you could recommend someone, and that things could be handled by phone."

Terri nodded as she gave the information sheet another look. "Do you realize how old that house is? It was deeded in 1806. If it's the original house, then it survived the War Between the States."

"I know it looks old. But I don't know anything except what I saw this morning. I've never had any contact with this part of the family. I don't even know why Anna Grayson would want to leave her property to me." The space between her brows pushed into a frown. "It isn't going to be a problem, is it? That it's so old? It has acreage."

"I haven't seen it yet. I'll drive out there today and take a look before I go home."

Dhari slumped against the back of the chair. "I was hoping this was going to be easy."

"I promise to make this as easy as I can." Terri offered a reassuring smile. "There is something, though, that you can do to help speed the process along."

"Name it, I'm there."

"Well, there are a couple of well-known architecture historians in the area that you could try to get an appointment with." Terri hesitated, then shook her head. "One would make you feel like you were trying to get an appointment with the Almighty, and the other would probably be more interested in inspecting your structure than he would the house. On second thought, I think it would be better, since the house dates back before the Civil War, to see if you can get in to see Dr. Hughes at the university. She's the most knowledgeable person I know on that era. She's lectured all over the country on the role of women during the Civil War. Smart lady. She can probably give you some background on the place, and she will be a whole lot more enjoyable to deal with."

"Whatever you think will help sell it."

"I need to be able to convince someone else to spend their money on a very old house out in the country that I don't know much about."

"I'll be at the university first thing Monday morning."

"Hang on a minute." Terri began flipping through a Rolodex as Dhari stood to leave. "Let me check out her schedule for Monday."

Efficient, apparently competent, and willing to work with my tight schedule. How lucky a choice was this? Dhari waited patiently for the first time since she'd left home. She watched as Terri Sandler neatly hand-printed the information from the other end of the phone conversation.

"Yes, thank you. And she has no problem with someone sitting in on a lecture? Yes, uh, huh. Wonderful. And you'll leave a message for her. Dhari, D-h-a-r-i, Weston. Thank you, you've been very helpful." Terri hung up the phone with one hand while opening a file drawer with the other. She lifted a manila folder and removed a copy of an area map. "Okay," she said, "this is how to get to the university." She highlighted the streets in yellow. "And I'll write directions to the building you want here on the back."

Dhari smiled. "I've never dealt with anyone as organized as you."

Terri's laughter was so contagious that Dhari began to laugh without even knowing why.

"Organized," Terri managed as her laughter tapered to a chuckle, "is not the description my friends use."

"Well, that's the one I'll be using."

Terri was still smiling. "And it's appreciated, believe me. Now, you don't have to sit in on the lecture if you feel pressed for time. But it might prove interesting. She has a break afterwards and she'll be expecting you."

"Thank you, Terri," Dhari said extending her hand. "I'm sorry this is such a convoluted mess."

"It's all in how you look at it. Give me a call Monday."

Chapter 3

Any concern about being conspicuous disappeared the instant Dhari entered the lecture hall. The room was so large that even minutes before lecture time she had her choice of a number of empty seats. She chose a seat in the middle of a row near the back.

The feeling was good, as comfortable as when she was the age of the students surrounding her. Maybe better. No stressful note taking, no need to worry about exams. She would just relax while some woman, mired in a century-old bloodbath, bores her into a guiltless daydream. The perfect classroom experience.

Dhari reached into the backpack nestled between her feet and turned off her cell phone in compliance with the sign above the chalkboard. The young woman in the seat next to her was busy reading. Dhari scanned the room. There were others reading as well, and others readying notebooks or talking. The majority of the students were young women. I could do this again, she thought. A class or two at a time and even exams wouldn't be so bad. I could take the web site classes and market myself up and out of a no-extra-money job. What would I lose? Two weeks of vacation time—much of which I'll use up dealing with this mess down here anyway? Won't miss what vacation time I never had.

The sound of miscellaneous conversation changed abruptly to hushed wonderings as three young men dressed in Civil War attire entered and stood at the front of the room. The sloped floor made it easy to see even from the back and Dhari watched intently as the first of the three approached the microphone.

"In September of 1861," he said, removing a faded kepi and tucking it inside a Confederate jacket that would have better fit a larger man, "my father and two older brothers and I left our farm and joined the Missouri State Guard to protect our way of life. My mother and sisters and grandfather, along with our loyal slaves continued to work the farm while we were away. I was the only one to return."

The second man stepped forward and removed his cap. He was dressed in a full Union blue uniform with a leather bag strapped to his side. "I was an apprentice at a newspaper in Baltimore. The information coming back from the early battles was sketchy and terribly outdated by the time we received it. I saw that my skills as a journalist could be put to much better use. When I enlisted in the militia my wife of six months would not leave my side. She traveled with our company and tended to the wounded."

The third soldier wore a long gray jacket and a nondescript leather hat with a large brim, and carried a long rifle. "I worked in a mercantile," he began, "for board and room for my mother, my sisters and me. My father had died of typhoid before the battle of Antietam. We had received no word from my brother for six months. When there was hope for a victory at Fredericksburg they called for volunteers to bolster the reinforcements. I enlisted and killed my first Union soldier as we pushed Burnside's forces to the north bank of the Rappahannock River. My company was never captured," he said, pulling off the leather hat to allow dark shoulder-length hair to fall from beneath it, "and we fought until the surrender. No one ever found out that I was a woman."

The room was filled with a hum of surprise that quieted only when Dr. Hughes emerged from a side aisle and addressed the class.

"The roles women played during the War Between the States, the Civil War, were even more varied than the sampling you just heard." She motioned toward the three soldiers. "Thank you to our drama students for so clearly making the point."

Dhari's first thought as the class applauded the actors out the door was that this woman wasn't the middle-aged, professor-type woman she had expected. No salt-and-pepper matronly styled hair, no below the knee two-piece suit or wire-rims on the end of her nose. Instead Dhari was watching an attractive thirty-something woman make a pair of jeans and a blazer look totally appropriate in a lecture hall.

Watching, she chided herself, not listening. Instead of concentrating and learning something, she was watching the sureness of Dr. Hughes's stride as she covered the distance back and forth across the front of the room. Her hands, too, kept Dhari's attention—sometimes clasped behind her back, sometimes tucked in a pants pocket, but most often cutting the air with emphasis. Their motion rounded her words with conviction and fanned them with a captivating passion.

Concentrate, Dhari reminded herself. There may not be a test, but she could ask you about the lecture later. What would you say, 'I didn't hear a word you said, I was too busy watching you?' The kind of fascination reminiscent of her college days when watching a woman teach was often more interesting than what she was teaching. Particularly classes that only an instructor could get excited about, and especially instructors that only she could get excited about. Dhari smiled and sat straighter in her seat. Unless she was mistaken, when this class was over she would be meeting her second southern dyke in as many days. Not a bad percentage.

"...a woman with a sizeable price on her head," Dr. Hughes was saying, "around $40,000 at one point, who not only served as a nurse during the Civil War, but a scout and a spy as well."

Damn. Who's she talking about? She glanced quickly at the

notes the girl sitting next to her was writing frantically. Harriet Tubman. You're damn lucky her handwriting is legible. No kidding, Harriet Tubman?

"Her involvement and incredible accomplishments with the Underground Railroad are well documented and more widely known than her role during the Civil War. With the lessons of the woods taught to her by her father as background, Harriet Tubman personally led nineteen rescue trips between Philadelphia and Maryland that brought three hundred slaves to freedom. Despite the danger magnified by the Fugitive Slave Act of 1850, Tubman never lost a slave and was never captured. It was reported that she carried a gun and made it clear that if any of them tried to turn back she would shoot them rather than jeopardize the mission."

With no understandable purpose, Dhari found herself jotting down an abbreviated account of the accomplishments on the back of the map Terri Sandler had given her.

"Astonishing as these accomplishments were, her heroics during the war produced even more amazing statistics. As a scout and spy for the Union army in South Carolina, Tubman helped to free over seven hundred and fifty slaves in one military campaign alone. There are few in history as worthy as she of the nickname of Moses. But despite three years of continuously risking her life for the Union, she was paid so little that she was virtually destitute after the war. It wasn't until 1897 that the government finally acceded to giving her a monthly pension of twenty dollars! That I'm sure allowed her to retire in grand style."

She smiled as the class groaned and added, "It seems she was valued more highly as a fugitive than she was as a hero." She motioned toward a portable chalkboard. "Which brings me to your assignment for next time. I want you to give a thoughtful analysis on what, if any, effect the attacks on the U.S. on September 11, 2001 had on that particular attitude. Was there a shift from 'bad boy' glorification, society's fascination with the likes of serial killers, to an appreciation of true heroes, or was the reaction due to fear and a need to feel safe?

Remember, I encourage you to discuss the subject with friends and classmates. No less than five pages, please. Have a great day."

In a manner of minutes the class had gathered their notebooks and backpacks and cleared the room, leaving Dr. Hughes collecting notes from the podium that she hadn't once referred to, and erasing the chalkboard.

"An astonishing woman," Dhari said as Dr. Hughes turned from the board, "Harriet Tubman."

Dhari was greeted with the same smile, bright and unpretentious, that had periodically lightened the lecture. "She empowers me anew every time I talk about her."

"A heroine to add to my list," Dhari returned. "At the top of which is Eleanor Roosevelt."

"Another favorite of mine as well, and a worthy candidate for the top of anyone's list."

"I'm sorry," she said extending her hand, "Dhari Weston. Thank you for letting me sit in today, Dr. Hughes. It was a very informative lecture." *At least the part I heard.*

"Dhari. What an interesting name. Where does it come from?"

"I have no idea. I've always assumed that I was stuck with it simply because my family had a fixation on 'D' names - Donna, Douglas, Grandma Dora, Aunt Deanna."

"It's wonderfully different." Then she added with a wink, "Be grateful that they didn't run out of girl names and you got stuck with Delbert."

Well, Dr. Hughes. You picked up more about the Westons than I intended to tell. "Yes," Dhari returned with a smile. "Delbert Weston might have been a hard career sell for me."

"Ah, unfortunately, the resumes would probably have a better chance with Delbert. But we all fight that battle." She started toward the door. "Where are you in the family hierarchy?"

Dhari kept stride. "Smack dab in the middle."

"The peace-maker." The doctor smiled. "So, what can I do for you, peace-maker Dhari?"

"Terri Sandler recommended you in hopes that you could give us some insight and advice on selling a piece of property I inherited."

"Dating back to my expertise I'm assuming."

"I don't mean to be presumptuous, but I'll only be here for a few days, and I really need some advice. If you normally receive a fee for this kind of thing, I'd be happy to pay you."

"I don't—"

Please.

"—charge a fee. How's tomorrow about four o'clock?"

"That would be perfect. Thank you, Dr. Hughes." They stopped beside a white Dodge Ram. "Shall I pick you up?"

"Look—"

The tone made Dhari frown.

"—I can't do this…" She tossed her case on the seat of the truck.

Dhari dropped her head.

"—unless you stop calling me Dr. Hughes." She smiled at the relief on Dhari's face. "I can't decide if it makes me sound stuffy or old—or both. I think Erin fits me better."

"I think the Doctor thing sounds intimidating," Dhari said with a little tilt of her head. "So, I'll be happy to call you Erin." She slipped her backpack strap over one shoulder. "Right here tomorrow?"

"I'm looking forward to it."

Dhari watched as Erin smiled, climbed into her truck, and pulled from the parking lot. A vision far from what she had expected an hour ago.

Chapter 4

"Maybe it's the company," Dhari was saying, "or maybe it's because I know where I'm going, but this time the drive out here seems less like a cross-country road trip."

Erin smiled absently. Springhill. Oh, my God! Springhill is the Grayson place. Where has my mind been? Incredible, she thought, staring out the car window. What are the odds that I'd be telling a direct Grayson heir what I know about her inheritance? And what do I know besides its place in history and the stories I've heard? A piece of architecture that by all accounts shouldn't have survived the most destructive war march on American soil. It doesn't seem like enough. If only I had made the time, followed my instincts. I could have met Anna Grayson, sat and talked with her, learned how a Grayson woman had owned her family's property for all those years. But I was too busy to do anything except drive slowly by, too busy giving lectures from books. Now a living piece of history is gone and what do I know?

Dhari's voice broke her thoughts. "How long have you been at the university?"

Erin turned from her stare at the countryside. "This is my fifth semester," she answered. "I haven't been in one place this long since college. I moved back two years ago when my mother was ill. We lost her shortly after."

"I'm sorry, Erin."

"They offered me a contract, so I took it partly for my dad. We really needed each other's support."

"No brothers or sisters?"

"No, just me—majorly spoiled and unconditionally loved." Erin returned her gaze quickly to the window. She blinked back what could have become a tear, and changed the subject. "So, why are you planning on selling? Hasn't your family always owned the property?"

"If they have owned it all these years then that makes it a very old family secret," Dhari replied. "Until a month ago, when a bank representative called me and said that my aunt had died and left me her estate, I didn't even know she existed."

"Well, she must have known that you existed."

"She never bothered to contact any of us. It doesn't make sense that someone I don't know would leave me everything she had."

"I'd be hooked," Erin replied. "I wouldn't be able to rest until I found out why."

"I'd like to know too, but there are way too many things that need my attention right now. I have to spend some extra time with my mother so that my dad can take part in a seminar at the college, find them the best supplemental health insurance, plan a birthday party for Mom, spend some time with my girlfriend so that she doesn't forget about me, and finish writing a grant for work by next Friday."

"Is that all?" Erin asked with a smile. "Shouldn't be a problem as long as you can run on caffeine and two hours of sleep a night."

"That's a scary thought. It sounds like my University of Michigan days all over again. Maize and blue and deadlines due."

Erin noted a hint of a smile from Dhari's profile. "Yeah, I wouldn't want to go there again, either. It didn't take me long to figure out that newfound freedom equated to newfound responsibilities." I wonder, Ms. Weston, what it will take to get a full-fledged smile from you. "So, who's the grant for?"

"Great Lakes AIDS Coalition. I'm in charge of project evaluations, and part of their grant writing team."

The car turned into the long drive. Erin remained silent all the way up, while her eyes were fixed on the house.

"American Georgian," she remarked as the car came to a stop at the top of the drive. "Maybe even virgin."

"Virgin?"

Erin's eyes never left the building as the women emerged from the car. Erin scanned it from roof to foundation. "Untouched," she said, walking toward the side of the house. She continued her assessment along the side yard with Dhari following. With a nod of her head she explained, "From what I can see it has remained unaltered over the years—no additions or deletions from the original structure." She nodded again. "Beautiful."

"Beautiful?" Dhari mumbled, looking more closely at her inheritance. "What am I missing here? Whatever beauty she sees isn't in the eye of this beholder."

"And this beech," Erin said with a turn toward the giant twisted trunk, "is a witness tree."

"Witness?"

Erin approached the tree, carefully stepping over protruding knurls of root and touched the smooth bark of a limb so contorted that it nearly touched the ground. "See how it has leaned for years out of the shadow of the house toward the sun? It's been here probably as long as the house has—a witness to all that has happened here."

"If only it could talk, right?"

Erin smiled. "'The wonder is that we see these trees and not wonder more', said Mr. Thoreau. I'm sure to the trained arborist it does talk. But this untrained mortal is just grateful to be able to see this piece of history close up."

Erin continued back around to the front of the house with

Dhari following. She gazed out over the overgrown yard and past the knoll. "Have you ventured out into the surrounding countryside?"

Dhari shook her head. "Haven't really had the time."

"There's a Civil War battleground not far from here. Part of Sherman's March," Erin explained. "This is just remarkable."

"Did you want to look at the inside?" Dhari asked.

"I'd love to if you'll let me come back at another time. I need to get back tonight. Structurally it should be a symmetrical plan," she looked at Dhari, "the building arranged around a central axis."

Dhari thought for a second and then nodded.

"I'll take a look at the plotting on the deed. I have enough to write some recommendations for you. Seeing the inside is merely personal curiosity."

"I'm not sure that I'll have to come back. I may be able to handle the rest by phone. But Terri Sandler will have a key and you are welcome to come out anytime and look around."

She's just walking away from this? Erin frowned and waited to make eye contact with Dhari. "I definitely will," she replied, wondering what stopped her from questioning the strange behavior.

"I want to thank you in advance for your recommendations," Dhari offered. "I appreciate you taking your time, and I wish you'd let me pay you."

"No," Erin said with a shake of her head. "That's not necessary." And the rest is none of my business, Erin decided. "A ride back into town is all I need," she said with a smile.

Chapter 5

Dhari retrieved the parking ticket from the dash of the RAV and settled herself comfortably in her own car. The familiarity was nice, no looking for buttons or hitting the windshield wipers when she needed the lights. She smiled at the ticket lady. "How are you doing? What a pretty day today," she said, paying for the parking and starting for I-94 and home.

It felt good to be back. For many that would be hard to say about Michigan in February. The sun low in a bright blue sky, reflecting off heavy white clouds and mounds of snow, teased Dhari into a deep breath of frigid air. She coughed and pulled the collar of her jacket up to protect the back of her neck from the five-below-zero wind chill. She retrieved her bag from the passenger seat and started for her apartment. Michigan was home, had been since Dhari was eight, and despite the occasional discomforts she was glad to be here.

Dhari stomped the salt from the treads of her boots just inside the door and took the stairs to her second floor apartment two at a time. An hour and a half, enough time to shower and almost relax before Jamie gets here. She quickly checked her Christmas cactus; the last of its fallen fuchsia blooms were long gone from the windowsill. It was her favorite plant and Jamie had remembered to water it just as she had promised.

Everything was in order as she whisked through the rooms leading to the bedroom. Thirty minutes to company. Dhari frowned at the concept. It's not compulsive, it's not even anal, really, it's just practical. A habit she had begun in college when time was at a premium. Do the task now; don't put it off. Keep things in order so that it would never take longer than thirty minutes to prepare for company. The practice still wanes occasionally while she fights the thought that it comes uncomfortably close to her mother's compulsions. Its benefits, however, are soon missed and, crazy or not, she begins the practice once again.

The bed had been made with clean sheets before she left, clean towels in the bathroom, and dishes done. She and Jamie would no doubt end up here for the night, so this is one of those times she'd risk being just a little crazy.

She tossed fresh black jeans on the bed, grabbed a shirt and sweater from a drawer and began to strip. "Shit." She muttered, racing to the other room to retrieve the ringing phone from her jacket.

Breathlessly she answered, "Hey, Dad. Yep, just got in. I was gonna jump in the shower then give you a call." She began unpacking her toiletries with her free hand. "Yep, good trip. Got everything done that I could. Everyone was very helpful...How's Mom?" She checked her watch and wriggled out of her underwear. "Uh, huh. I'll stop by after work tomorrow. I've got more questions now for Mom than when I left...well, I'm gonna ask them anyway. She must know something...okay...Yep, I know. What kind of shopping?" Dhari took a deep breath and let it out slowly as she listened. "Okay, I'll try to take her this week. Yes, I love you, too. See you tomorrow."

Dhari leaned her head back under the pulsating spray of the shower and tried to enjoy a few minutes of relaxation. She had to admit that being unavailable for the past few days had felt good, in a guilty kind of way. Tomorrow will come soon enough, along with a whole routine of responsibilities. And the questions, more than ever, will plague her thoughts.

How could Mom lose track of practically her whole family? It doesn't make sense. There's no excuse, she's not that crazy. Well, some days maybe she is. But enough to go all these years with no contact, no recognition of anyone past her mother?

The thought suddenly occurred that perhaps they lost track of her—on purpose. Grandma Em had always seemed normal enough, seriously religious, but nonmeddling and accessible. Had the rift started there, with something she had done? Had she judged someone unfairly or fought over a will or something? Could it be some pettiness that caused such irreparable damage? Maybe no one even knows anymore. Certainly Mother isn't offering any insight. It would be too easy to accept that if it hadn't been talked about all those years, it shouldn't be talked about now. A copout that always ended up butting heads with her concern that history was about to repeat itself. She hoped with all her heart that it would not, that pettiness and intolerance would be overcome and that understanding and love would be able to soothe the wounds. But her brother and sisters were well on their way to a similar separation from their mother. And as hard as Dhari had tried there didn't seem to be anything she could do to fix it.

Whenever she was with her family, she steered the conversations away from potential triggers, made sure the grandbabies didn't cry, and tried to keep the older kids occupied peacefully. But her efforts were often fruitless. If it was a bad day for her mother, Lela, it was a bad day, period. Anyone there on one of those days had to be prepared to steer clear and ignore, or leave and take a chance on another day. Hard enough for adults to do, but even harder for children.

Deanne, the youngest, was the only one of the Weston children who was not past the embarrassment-in-front-of-peers years so her absence was more easily excused. The absence of Douglas's sarcasm was too often a welcomed break. Donna and Dana had children to whom they had to explain grandma's weird and often hurtful ways. They had all reached the saturation point. It had become easier and more comfortable to just stay away. Each had developed their own ways of dealing with, or avoiding, their own dysfunctions and their mother's as well.

Douglas responded to everything with sarcasm and anger. Dana thought everything was disturbingly funny. Donna and Deanne merely disassociated, and Dhari tried to fix it all. None were particularly successful.

Therapy did seem to support Donna's distance, but to date it had done nothing for Douglas except turn a portion of his anger into more pointed sarcasm. Deanne, still in school, couldn't afford therapy. And Dhari, out of questionably sound respect for her mother's privacy, avoided it. Her alternative was to read everything applicable she could find. Was she manic-depressive as the doctor said? What about the compulsions—straightening the fringe on the rug until Dad got rid of it, scrubbing the sink until the enamel was gone? The diagnosis certainly didn't address all the symptoms, and neither did the treatment. The discussions among the siblings still always came to the same conclusion—their father had an ironclad psyche of unknown origin, and their mother needed another go at analysis and treatment. All but Dhari, however, had given up on trying to get her there.

I'm not going to be the one who wishes I had tried a little harder or been patient just a bit longer. They'll have to live with their regrets some day, but not me. Dhari stepped from the shower and pulled her towel from the hook. Not me.

Dhari checked her watch, although she knew before looking that Jamie was late. It was rare that she wasn't. She picked up the copy of *SportsWoman* from the table, collapsed onto the couch and began fighting the suspicions that always haunted her after a half an hour of waiting.

Just late as usual, nothing to worry about. She flipped through the magazine, reading the captions beneath the pictures and a short paragraph here and there. Longer articles were mentally bookmarked for another time when she would remember what she had read. Corralling a wandering mind wasn't a simple task. She had trained herself to focus on the ball as it leaves the pitcher's hand and follow it to contact with her bat; she had practiced until she could see the ball into her glove no matter how hard it had been hit or how many times it had taken a bad, and painful, hop in the past. With practice, she could do this too.

She replaced the magazine so that its top edge formed a perfect triangle with the corner of the table, then arranged the pillows neatly against the back of the couch so that each slightly overlapped the last. When she realized what she was doing she picked up an armful of pillows and tossed them haphazardly back onto the couch, then pushed the magazine askew.

Dammit! I will not be my mother's daughter.

The buzzer saved the remainder of the room from her reaffirming. She hit the button and opened the door as Jamie bounded up the steps.

"Hey, Babe," she said, hardly out of breath, "I'm not too late, am I?"

That depends on whose definition of late we're using. Dhari checked her watch again. "We'll miss the first show, but we could eat first then go to the ten o'clock."

"We could," Jamie said, standing to her full height and closing the distance between them. "Or..." she slid her hands around Dhari's waist and pulled her close. "I could show you that I missed you."

Dhari's forehead rested against Jamie's cheek. She didn't immediately raise her head to the kiss she knew was waiting.

"Hey," Jamie said softly as she lifted Dhari's chin. "You want to see the movie that badly?"

The scents of Nike Cologne and freshly shampooed hair, pure and untainted by cigarette smoke and alcohol, quickly negated her hesitation. "No, it's okay. I guess it was just the sudden change of plans." It sounded illogical the moment she uttered it. With Jamie no plan was set in stone. "I missed you, too," she said, pressing her lips to Jamie's and welcoming the arousal it caused. What could be more exciting than Jamie Bridgewater wanting you? What else could ever feel this good? Questions that needed no answer beyond the flush of her skin as lips coveted by so many others fused with her own. They pressed and parted, and the heat turned to wetness. Mental want become physical response. The quicker the hands worked beneath her sweater on the buttons of her shirt, the quicker her heart beat.

The thought occurred suddenly that they would not get as far as the clean sheets on the bed—then it was gone. It was replaced by maneuvering backward around the coffee table, wriggling from as much clothing as she could while keeping Jamie's hands moving over her body, rubbing over the front of her jeans.

She felt the edge of the couch against the back of her legs, Jamie's tongue deep in her mouth, and intense heat from the hand rubbing the seam along the crotch of her jeans. This is where she wanted to be, consumed by sensation, deep in need. No room for fear or worry, no time for self-analysis. No need for thought at all.

She gave up her thoughts as she gave up her body—delivering it willingly into Jamie's hands. She moved with urgency beneath her on the couch, widening her legs, lifting her hips with a frantic rhythm that now matched the groping of their tongues.

As she always did, Jamie rode her quickly to a state of demand, pushing her thigh and her hips up between Dhari's legs, showing no mercy for breathless gasps, allowing not a moment for words to form. Jeans pushed against jeans, sliding, grinding. Cool hands and the heat of Jamie's mouth searched and covered and manipulated the bare flesh of Dhari's breasts until she could take no more. She forced her hand between the tightness of their hips, fumbled open the zipper of her pants, grabbed Jamie's hand and forced it between her legs. Dhari's desperate cry was answered immediately as Jamie's fingers slid into the wetness. All she could do then was clutch Jamie tightly to her and drive her hips upward as the desperation exploded too quickly into orgasm.

Again and again she thrust her hips upward, trying to prolong the intensity of it, grasping every last bit of fulfillment. Then she allowed them to sink back down onto the cushions, squeezing her thighs firmly around Jamie's hand, holding her there until the quivering stopped.

That it ended too soon was barely a thought. She knew not to even let it form because as soon as her body recovered she knew Jamie would skillfully coax her there again—and again, as long as mind and body were willing. And only at Dhari's insistence did she allow the favor to be returned.

There was never any doubt that she was well loved. Dhari pressed her lips into the fresh smell of Jamie's hair and thought of how pleased she was that they had stayed here tonight.

Chapter 6

The Weston house was a typical little wood and brick ranch that formed many of Saline's subdivisions in the sixties and seventies. Small, easily maintained yards and manageable taxes made it the hands down choice when Jerry Weston had to move his family. Diligence and a degree of sacrifice that allowed few luxuries paid off the mortgage, and now there seemed little reason to move. Ironically, the vacations and travel that were possible now couldn't be enjoyed as a family, and Lela's mood could rarely be counted on. It made Dhari sad to see the years of hard work go unrewarded.

Dhari started to pull into the narrow driveway before she realized that her father wasn't home from work yet. She backed out and parked on the street, but fought the temptation to go have a Coke and wait until he was home. Her mother's moods were so unpredictable that sometimes it was better to spend time with her alone and other times it was better to have her dad there to keep the conversation on an even keel. Today, who knows?

She grabbed the envelope of papers and pictures from her aunt's house and headed for the side door.

"Mom," she called, her head just inside the door, "it's Dhari."

"Don't you track that mud in here," Lela Weston shouted.

So much for comfortable and realistic. She removed her shoes and sighed as her mother rounded the corner of the kitchen. "It's dry out, Mom, no new snow. I'm in my socks." A response that was as automatic as it was futile.

"You do this on purpose. You wait until I've worked all day cleaning the floors," her face was flushed with anger. "You and your father, you do it to me on purpose. It's mean, it's just mean."

I should have waited. When will I finally learn to trust my gut? "The floor looks great, Mom." She tried to embrace her mother, but she shrugged her off.

"Someday I'm going to stop being the maid around here and have a life. No one appreciates it anyway."

"We appreciate all your hard work. Dad especially appreciates it. But we've told you, Mom, you do way more than you need to. There are no kids to mess it up, and you have to admit Dad's pretty neat for a guy. Use the time to do things you want to do." Advice still given and still unable to be heeded.

"Like your dad does?"

Here we go. Dhari hung her jacket and held up the envelope. "Mom, I've got some pictures I want to show you."

"Where do you think he is right now? That old bastard."

"Mom!"

"With his whore, that's where."

"Stop it, now. I'm not going to stay here and listen to this. You know he's got a department meeting tonight. It's been the second Thursday of the month for ten years."

"You think I'm paranoid. Everyone thinks I'm paranoid. But I know what's going on. I've got proof. Come in here with me," she insisted. "I'll show you." She marched down the hall toward what had become a catchall room. "Your dear father," she muttered.

Dhari let out a heavy breath and followed. How in the hell have they stayed together? Why in the hell have they stayed together?

Lela opened the closet, removed boxes and bags from the corner and turned to hand Dhari a shoebox. "I found where he hides the letters. He thinks he's so clever."

In that moment it seemed a real possibility. Her father was at that vulnerable time in his life; he was a better than average looking man with a pleasant personality, and he certainly had cause enough to stray. It was one of those moments, and there had been many over the years, when sorting the truth from the irrational was so difficult. With a track record that was less than perfect, Dhari proceeded cautiously, trying not to jump to one conclusion or the other. She opened the box and examined the contents. There were no envelopes, only neatly folded letters. She unfolded the first one.

Dammit, Mother. She unfolded the second, and the third. Damn myself. Clinging to something that's not there. "Mom, these are letters you wrote to Dad. Look," she said pointing to the bottom of the letter, "right here, 'Your Sweet Pea'. That's you. And the dates—did you see the dates?"

"He thinks he's so clever, having her use my nickname, using fake dates. But I knew, even before I found these. It's not one of his students falling for their history professor; oh, no, they're too flighty. No, this is the same one for a long time now. He's no playboy, your father; he wants his mistress always there for him."

"Mom, that's nonsense. Look at these. Read them through again. Maybe you'll remember that you said these things. Like this, 'I missed you more than usual today, my darling. I walked through the park during lunch; there were so many couples talking and holding hands. I was jealous of them. I couldn't stop thinking that that should be us right now. How long will it be? I miss you so.'"

Lela was shaking her head. "No, I don't want to hear anymore."

"This must have been the summer he studied in Europe." Dhari continued scanning another letter. "Here, Mom. See if you remember this. 'My friend, Elaine, called today; we're going—'"

"No," Lela shouted. "I won't listen to his whore's words. No more."

"These are your words, your letters. Let me keep reading; you'll recognize some people or places. That'll prove it to you. Just let me try."

Lela snatched the letters from Dhari's hands. "I know what I know."

"This is—" Don't say it. "This is nonsense, Mom, pure nonsense. You're worried about nothing. Dad is a good man. He loves you or he would have been gone long ago." She looked into her mother's eyes, hoping to see some relief from her words, but there was none. "Okay, I'll tell you what, we'll go right now and meet Dad after his meeting. We'll surprise him and then go to dinner. You'll see he'll be right where he's supposed to be."

"Take his side," Lela shouted, her face red with anger. "Lie for him. He's a bastard and you're just as bad as he is. I hate you both."

"Hate?" Dhari shouted back. "You hate me? Listen to yourself. You want support? You want validation? How is that possible? You want me to validate your craziness? Is that what you want?"

Without warning Lela struck out, slapping Dhari hard across the face. "Don't talk to me that way," she said, shaking with anger. "Get out of my house."

Dhari turned; hurt and anger propelled her through the house. She grabbed her jacket and shoes, not stopping to put them on, and flung the storm door open so hard that it sprung the closure.

She started her car and drove to the end of the block before she realized how severely her body was shaking. She turned the corner, pulled over to the curb and turned off the engine. She slammed the palm of her hand hard against the steering wheel. Tears streamed down her cheeks.

"I can't do this anymore...God!" she shouted at the top of her voice, "I can't do it!" She bounced her head back against the headrest. "I can't help you." Tears continued uncontested. "I can't help anyone. I can't even help myself."

Dhari closed her eyes, tried to wall up the hurt, to hide it from herself. She visualized the blocks, mortaring them in place one by one. But her face still stung from the force of her mother's hand and the wall crumbled. It's no use. It's never any use. "Why can't you be normal?" she yelled. "Why do you have to be so damn crazy?" You never loved me—you never could. "You never could."

She remained there, eyes closed, until the tears stopped and her body finally relaxed. She knew there was only one person who could really make a difference, and it was clear that that was where her hope rested.

Dhari parked next to her father's car in the community college parking lot and waited. He was right here where he was supposed to be. He'd always been the one thing she could count on. Only once had she doubted him; long ago, before she realized the depth of her mother's problems. Anxious and fearful of what she might find she had followed and watched him for over a week. All she got for her effort was guilt for not having trusted him. Her mother's accusations, as convincing as they had sounded, were unfounded and her fears based on some internal set of circumstances that had no apparent reality. It had been almost as devastating to come to that conclusion, as it would have been to have found her father cheating. Sadly, dealing with a father's infidelity, or even divorce, may have been easier than dealing with whatever was going on in her mother's head.

Yet, here she was again. Because she doubted her own trust in him? Or because she was secretly hoping for some tiny bit of proof of her mother's sanity. If there was something, a close friendship with a female teacher, an emotional attachment that never went any further, it could explain an intuition that merely got blown out of proportion. That would be reason-able, excusable. Sometimes we just know things, sense things, are able to feel that things aren't right by how someone reacts to even unrelated situations. Pettiness, anger, impatience could be a need to justify; and the opposite, saintly patience

33

and understanding could be tip-offs of guilt. That's all she needed, just a reason, a rational reason for suspicion. Then she could accept that her mother's fears had caused her to overreact, and at least some of her behavior would be understandable. But she hadn't found that reason, probably because one didn't exist, and when she stopped feeling and hoping and reacting she knew that looking for it was irrational.

"That looks like my daughter's car," remarked Jerry Weston, as he and two colleagues walked the sidewalk next to the parking lot.

"Would that be the princess, the sugar plum, or the—?"

"Dhari," Jerry said with a smile.

"The healthcare saint," his colleague chided.

"Hey, Jerry," the other man interjected, "you're a proud man, and rightly so. John here would be just as proud if he could ever find a woman that wanted to have his children."

Jerry laughed affably with the men. "I'm a pretty lucky ole duff." He looked toward the car parked next to his own. "Dhari has a gilded heart. A lot of people depend on her, including me. I don't know what I'd do without her." He gave a pat to John's shoulder and added. "I guess that's a sign that I'm getting old."

Muffled voices caught Dhari's attention. She opened her eyes as her father said goodnight to his colleagues. Guys, just as she would have expected. No women colleagues even close enough for suspicion. She rolled down her window and called to him as he neared the car.

"Dhari, honey," he said with a smile.

"Can I talk to you for a few minutes?"

"Of course. What's wrong?" He removed the brown leather cap he always wore during the cold months and slid into the passenger's seat. "Did you stop at the house?"

"I went over early to show Mom some pictures and stuff." The tone of her voice was enough to tell him that things had not gone well.

"She forgot that I had a staff meeting," he concluded.

"She didn't forget, Dad. You've got to stop denying that she's in trouble. How can you possibly..." He looked her straight in the eye and she realized, "It's not denial, is it? You make it sound better than it is for my benefit."

"Sometimes she's fine," he returned. "She loves you very much, she loves all of you kids."

"She just slapped me across the face and told me that she hated me, and you."

"Oh, God, honey." He took Dhari's hand and patted it between his own. "I'm sorry. You know she doesn't mean that. She's just upset."

"She's not upset, she's not nervous. She's ill, and she needs treatment. All these years, Dad, it's only gotten worse. I can't take it anymore. This was it today. I mean it this time. Unless she gets help I won't be around."

"You know it doesn't do any good to bring it up while she's feeling like this." He turned his attention to a car driving by in front of them. "And when she's feeling good I hate bringing it up because it just hurts her. I don't like to do anything to spoil her good days."

Dhari waited for his eyes to come back to her. "I know this may sound harsh, and I don't say it to hurt you, but unless you find a way to convince her, you're going to lose what's left of the family." She watched him pull his eyes from her and nod. "Find a way, Dad. Please."

Chapter 7

Douglas Weston was shoveling the last of the daylong snow from the top of his driveway when Dhari pulled in. Still in his brown UPS uniform he hadn't been home long. He leaned the shovel against the house, quickly packed two baseball-sized snowballs and pelted Dhari as she opened the car door.

"You shithead," she yelled, wiping snow from her face and bolting after him. "You've had it. I don't care how big you are."

He was laughing and running as if he were twelve. She was chasing and yelling as if she were, too. She plowed through the knee-high mound next to the drive, snow pushing up over her boots and under her pant legs, and chased him across the little front yard. He pushed through the low boughs of the big pine that hid the corner of the house. Dhari held up her hands to keep them from slapping back into her face, but didn't slow her pursuit.

The harder he laughed, the more determined she became. He cleared the neighbor's drive and its boundary of knee-high snow with long strides while Dhari crashed through it to add still more to the cold wetness in her boots. But it didn't faze her. She would catch him if she had to chase him all the way to Detroit.

"Forget it," he yelled, "I'm having lunch already."

"Pack it up, Dough Boy," she returned, a childhood putdown that bore no resemblance to the now lanky frame.

He turned his head to see that she was indeed close behind, and in doing so he misjudged a turn around the corner of the neighbor's house. His right foot failed to plant firmly and slid to the left underneath him. He was face down in the snow in an instant.

Dhari pounced on him immediately, her full weight in the center of his back. The sudden weight forced the air from his lungs with a painful sounding cough, but Dhari showed no mercy. As fast as she could she grabbed the collars of his jacket and shirt and began shoving handfuls of cold, wet snow down his back. His shoulder blades squeezed back sharply and his back arched.

"Ahhh," he said loudly. "Fester! Fester!"

She honored his surrender by dropping the last handful of snow, but intentionally placed her hands over the lump of snow in his jacket and mashed it down as she rose. He countered by grabbing her leg before she could step clear and flipping her on her back.

"Oh," she managed with a thud, "no honor."

"I'm sorry." Douglas rolled onto his back next to her. "I couldn't resist. Claim my dessert."

"Claimed." Dhari dropped her guard and smiled to herself. Sometimes she wished they could both go back and be Dough Boy and Pan again, running the rooftops, making secret pacts, and vowing never to grow up. They counted on each other then, from tag-team wrestling against any challengers to keeping each other's secrets. To this day no one else knows that it was Douglas and his friends who rolled Mrs. Campbell's Volkswagen Beetle onto its top in her driveway, leaving her to find it like a turtle on its back in the morning. And no one except Douglas knows that Dhari at fifteen was crawling out the window of her basement bedroom after midnight to meet Kay Logen. Three years older and a known lesbian, Kay Logen was off limits, and for good reason if you're worried about your daughter finding solace and excitement and her first sexual experience in the arms of another woman. Nothing could have stopped the pounding of the hammer in her chest or the meltdown that started at merely the thought of what they would do, the meltdown that traveled through her innards and pooled between her legs. Nothing could have stopped her from finding a way of getting to Kay and the magical heat that she created. And if Douglas didn't give her up then, she figured he never would.

"Hey," she said, looking skyward, "do you know you have a badminton racket sticking out of your eaves trough?"

"Yeah. That was the last time Lisa beat me. I left it up there on purpose."

Dhari thumped him on the chest with the back of her hand.

"I know," Douglas acknowledged. "But it wasn't the losing. It was the damn neighbor behind us. We couldn't enjoy playing in our own yard without him sitting there in his lawn chair, drinking his Buds and riding me like a bronco buster."

"Is that the same guy who piles his dog's poop in the corner near your grill?"

"Yeah. I think pushing my buttons takes the place of sex for him."

"And you lost it anyway?"

"I didn't hop the fence and make a Popsicle out of him with my racket."

Dhari laughed until Douglas joined her.

"That's a visual I could have done without." She held her hand up. He intertwined their fingers and clasped it in the air. "But, hey, you didn't cross over."

"Our pact's still good?"

"Always. I'm counting on you. If I ever cross over—."

"Don't worry," he said, squeezing her hand hard and then releasing it. "I'll tell you."

They lay there, silently watching giant white billows gradually cover the sky above.

"It has to be at the very first sign."

He nodded beside her.

"Otherwise we'll be too crazy to believe each other."

He raised his hand again and she clasped it. "The very first sign," he promised.

There was silence for a moment, then Dhari asked, "Does Lisa know about our pact?"

"No. She would think the pact was crazy."

"Is it?"

"Only to COSP's."

Dhari returned a blank look.

"Children Of Sane Parents," he explained.

She nodded. "Are you going to marry Lisa?"

"I would have to grow up. She would never have a conversation with me lying in the snow."

"She hasn't left."

"She will."

"Then why are you with her?"

"For the same reason that you're with Jamie."

She was beginning to feel the cold from the snow now seeping through the layers and getting uncomfortably close to her skin. It seems that she had shortchanged the benefits of his therapy. She shivered but made no attempt to get up. He would tell her what he thought regardless. That's why he was the only one that the pact would work with.

"Neither one of us is going to chance going crazy on a spouse."

"But we still go through the motions."

He assumed, "Of trying to make things work?"

She nodded.

"We're trying to keep them here as long as possible. Think about it. We're scared. Admitting the truth is accepting that we will inevitably be alone in our craziness."

"I don't want to think about that."

"I guess that's why you're not as cynical as I am, you don't let yourself think about it."

"Maybe we're already crossing over," she said with a

shiver. "Lying here in the snow like this can't be normal."

"Come on," he said, jumping up and pulling her with him. "One of us has to stay sane long enough to tell the other they're going crazy." He put his arm around her shoulders as they trudged back to the house.

Chapter 8

What the hell she was doing back on a plane to Atlanta Dhari couldn't say. Curiosity? Dangerous. Did it really kill the cat? Or worse, an anal inability to give up control of the situation? Even more dangerous. She covered her feverish forehead with the cool palm of her hand. She couldn't think about it right now.

Ignoring the onset of subtle symptoms did nothing to keep the flu from hitting her full force as soon as the plane was airborne. The annoying dry sensation at the base of her nasal cavity had been replaced with a distinct soreness. The pressure from the increased elevation resulted in a horrendous headache and excruciating pain in both ears. She pushed her jacket into the crevice between the seat back and the window, gingerly pressed her head into the soft down and closed her eyes. The voices of the couple next to her became distant and muffled, and her body began to perspire. She rode out the trip in misery without the benefit of sleep.

By the time Dhari dragged herself through the airport, picked up the rental car and made the drive to the house, it was all she could do to unlock the door and climb the stairs to the bedroom. She pulled back the feather duvet, removed only her shoes, and slipped her aching body between the cool sheets. There were no thoughts of reports, or finding an auctioneer, no thoughts of time constraints or work or Jamie. She could think of nothing except how awful she felt and burying herself deep beneath the covers until the warmth took the chills from her body. It had been years since she had been this sick.

Dhari shivered and pulled the covers she was clenching tightly beneath her chin up over her head. Her hair and everything touching her body was drenched in sweat. The brief exchange of air started the chills again. She began to move uneasily, rubbing her feet against each other, alternately stretching one leg and then the other, then pulling her knees into a fetal position. Nothing helped. Her body ached at every joint; the rubbing hurt her skin. She didn't know what time it was or what day it was. She only knew that she was very sick and very thirsty. Her last attempt at water, however, had ended up in the toilet and the acid from the vomit made her throat so sore that she began spitting into a wad of tissues to avoid swallowing.

There was nothing she could do except try to calm herself and hope for sleep. She was left to her own resources, just as she had been most of her growing up years. Her mother, there all day, was distant and easily upset by the mess and unable to comfort her. It was up to her father to do what he could when he came home from work. He would get her to eat, pin her hair back with a barrette and wash her face. And when it looked like more than a cold, he was the one who bundled her up and took her to the clinic. She could remember thinking just a little longer, go to sleep and pretty soon he'll be home. Thinking it over and over got her through, and always the smell of him, like starched collars and fresh-mowed grass, rushing into the stale room made her feel better.

There was only one memory, and it had to be from when she was very young, that it was her mother's hands, cool and comforting, on her flushed face. A short, almost forgotten, memory of being held in her mother's arms until she fell asleep. She wondered if it was real. Maybe she had just wished it into a memory.

She awakened to someone moving about the room. Startled, Dhari dropped the blanket from her head to find Nessie Tinker staring back at her.

"Child, ya can't beat dem chills in dem wet clothes. Here now," she said, spreading a quilt over the chair by the bed, "get outta dem tings. Leave em right dere in da bed. Put dese on," she ordered, handing her the pajamas she'd pulled from the bag Dhari had left on the floor. "Den sit over here."

Too sick to do anything but cooperate, Dhari shed her wet clothes, donned the dry pajamas and crawled out of bed. As she sat in the chair, Nessie pulled the quilt over Dhari's head and wrapped it around her like a papoose. The warmth was immediate. "Thank you," she whispered, but Nessie was already busy stripping the bed.

Although not much taller than the footboard, she pulled everything from the bed with remarkable ease. All except the stripped pillows and the duvet went into a huge pile on the floor. By the time Dhari opened her eyes again the bed was freshly made and Nessie was backing out the bedroom door pulling a pile of linens nearly as big as her. She wanted to tell her to stop but anything above a whisper hurt her throat too much.

Cool hands soothed her forehead and cheeks like the memory she didn't trust. Dhari opened her eyes. Nessie brushed the now dry hair away from Dhari's face and held her hand to her forehead again.

"Fever broke," she said. "Gotta take some fluids now."

Dhari shook her head slowly from side to side. "Can't keep it down," she whispered. "And my throat burns."

"Shhh, jes trust ole Nessie."

Dhari smiled and closed her eyes. No teeth on top. It had been the first time she'd been close enough to notice. No wonder she sounds like that, no teeth on top. It was the 'shhh' that gave it away. Well that's all right then, Nessie, she decided. That's all right.

Dhari propped herself up and accepted the hot mug without protest.

"Ain't too hot, tested it myself. Herbs in da tea will soothe da burning. Slippery elm bark and licorice root, you'll see."

A tentative sip proved that it was indeed just right. Dhari took a bigger swallow, then another. The heat felt surprisingly good on her throat. If only I can keep it down.

"Here, eat dis." Nessie broke off a small bite of burned toast, soaked it in a bowl of hot tea and stuck it in Dhari's mouth. "Okay, more tea," she ordered.

She continued like that, soaking the pieces and feeding them to Dhari until both the toast and the tea were gone.

She put her hand on Dhari's forehead and gently pushed her back to the pillow. "Gonna feel much better now, you'll see." She smoothed her hand down Dhari's cheek and held it there for a few seconds, then nodded. "Sleep now, child. I'll be right here."

And she was there, only a few feet away, sitting in the chair reading every time Dhari woke up.

"Nessie, what time is it?"

"Yer feeling better I see," the old woman replied. She looked closely in the dim light at a watch too large for her wrist. "Close on eight o'clock."

"Sunday night?"

"Monday."

Dhari sat up too quickly. She groaned and clutched her head. Although the body aches had ceased, her headache had not. "Why did this have to happen now when I have so much to do?"

"Maybe it's God slowin' ya down, turnin' ya around."

Another groan. "When did you come in? I lost track."

"Didn't see no light up here Saturday night." She motioned toward the window by the bed. "Figured sometin' was wrong."

"I feel bad that you changed the bed—what, three times? You washed my face, got fluids in me, fed me," she looked into the waiting eyes, "and stayed with me. And I just let you."

"I weren't askin' permission. And dere weren't no need in you askin'."

"You took care of me like that without even knowing me."

"I got all the knowin' I need."

Chapter 9

Except for the cough, which had become increasingly insistent during the night, Dhari felt almost human this morning. She stood before the bedroom window, arched her back and stretched her shoulders. Cautiously she breathed the air, warmed by the morning sun flooding through the partially opened window, and suddenly realized what fresh meant. No exhaust fumes, no factory omissions. The air smelled rainwashed clean. She felt a brief twinge of exhilaration, of invulnerability, before she dared a deeper breath that had to be stopped short at the tick in the back of her throat. The muscles in her abdomen tightened in preparation for another coughing spell, but Dhari cleared her throat until the urge subsided.

Even without another deep breath the aroma from the kitchen made its way past the reddened tip of her nose, gathered, and titillated an olfactory sense that Dhari nearly forgot she had. As she pulled her softest, most comfortable sweatshirt over her head, the combination of smells started a painful rumbling in her stomach. "I am so hungry," she muttered, fluffing unruly ends of freshly washed hair. "I don't even care if it comes back up."

She hurried too quickly to the top of the stairs, and felt the weakness from three days in bed in her legs as she descended.

Quiet voices greeted her as she made her way through the narrow hallway toward the kitchen. Nessie's voice, high and light, was unmistakable, but it wasn't until Dhari peered through the doorway that she realized the second one belonged to Erin Hughes.

Her immediate reaction was to turn and slip quietly back up the stairs and shut herself in the bedroom. It was bad enough that Nessie had seen her in her most disgusting state. That had been beyond her control. Surely no one could hold her responsible for that; if it had been possible, of course, she never would have allowed it. That parents and siblings had been at times subjected to each other in less than appealing states was circumstance. They had no choice. Nessie, however, did. Why she would choose to care for someone, a stranger, in such a nasty state was beyond Dhari's comprehension.

And her state today wasn't a whole lot better. Clean was the best that could be said, and that was overshadowed by the obvious—pale, drawn, disheveled and weak. Not the picture you want to present to the world, or more specifically, to Dr. Hughes.

Dhari leaned against the wall, the quivering in her legs making the trip back up the stairs less appealing. But she couldn't force herself through the doorway. Her stomach rumbled so loudly that she feared it could be heard in the kitchen. How irrational is it to demand that a weak, starving body go without food or rest because of how it looked? She looked down the hallway toward the stairs. The impulse was overwhelming. They don't know I'm down here. Don't know whether or not I'm too sick to join them. Would never know. But if she did go back up she would have to call Douglas. She'd have to discuss how closely this resembles her mother's compulsions. Cleaning floors and walls and counters, late into the night, with one cleaning product after another. Driving herself to exhaustion and anger. For what purpose? To be presentable. But to whom?

Dhari listened again for the voices still drifting softly from the kitchen. She pushed from the wall and turned toward the doorway.

Erin greeted her with a smile as Dhari entered the kitchen. "Well, good morning. How are you feeling?"

Dhari tried to tuck uncooperative sprigs of hair behind her ear. "Like I've just risen from the dead. But, thanks to Nessie, a whole lot better than I look." She flattened the front of her sweatshirt against her torso. "I must have lost ten pounds. It feels like my stomach is flapping up against my backbone."

"Gonna fix dat. Sit down here," Nessie directed.

"Ever had a real southern breakfast?" Erin asked.

Dhari began to answer but started coughing instead. When she was in control again she shook her head.

"You're in for a genuine treat, then. Nessie's fixed biscuits and gravy, and sausage, and grits. It's all I can do to honor my sweet southern mother and sit here and visit without digging in."

"You should have gone ahead," Dhari said as Nessie placed a steaming plate in front of her. "Or, yelled at me. I didn't know you were here."

"I don't have a class until this afternoon. And since you offered, I thought I'd come out and take you up on your invitation to see the inside." She thanked Nessie with a smile as her breakfast was served. "As it turned out I have had the beginning of a wonderful conversation with Nessie." She watched Dhari politely attacking her breakfast. "You know she is the best resource you could ever find on this place."

"Told her dat right off," Nessie said, settling in a chair.

Dhari hesitated for a moment, then touched her forehead and looked away. "Yes, you did." She made brief eye contact with both of them. "You must think I'm a real bubblehead."

"Actually, I'm glad you didn't realize it sooner. I've learned more from Nessie in an hour and a half than I learned from any class I've taken."

"You're thanking fate for my air bubble?" Dhari tried to laugh but coughed instead.

Erin smiled. "You bet."

"All dat happens, happens fer a purpose."

"I don't see any purpose in my getting sick. All that did was waste time and money. I'm no closer to selling this place than I was before I came. I'll be out of vacation days before I get it on the market." Dhari reached for another biscuit. "Oh, Nessie, this is the best breakfast I think I've ever had. Thank you."

"And I second that," Erin added.

Nessie only nodded and continued eating.

"What time do you have to be at the airport?"

"Four-thirty."

"When will you be coming back?"

"Terri Sandler has the name of an auctioneer she's recommending, so hopefully I can take care of everything by phone until the house sells. Actually, I guess I don't even have to be here for the closing."

Erin looked up in surprise. "Are you just going to auction all the contents without going through everything?"

Dhari hadn't really thought about how anyone else but Jamie might react to her decisions regarding this place. She was slow to reply. "I didn't know Anna Grayson, so nothing here has sentimental value." She hesitated but there was no reply. Erin's eyes never left her. Nessie was slowly finishing the remainder of her breakfast. "I have a small apartment. Even if I found something that I was tempted to keep..."

Erin blotted her lips with her napkin and leaned back in her chair. "What about personal things that should be kept in the family? Photos or papers, things that could teach you something about this part of your family?"

Dhari rose from the table and began gathering the empty plates. "I'm not sure I want to know." Not until she reached the sink did she realize how that must have sounded. She turned to explain. "I'm not saying that Ms. Grayson wasn't worth knowing, I'm sure she was. It's just that something caused my grandmother to detach herself from her mother and sister, and I question whether knowing why would be beneficial." Too much talking caused her to start coughing again. She turned away and coughed into her napkin. A crazy relative, or two, down the line? Or was it incest, inbreeding? Was it as common as they say? Would knowing really make any difference?

"Sorry about this cough," she said facing them again. "It must be annoying."

Nessie rose and started in the direction of the back door. "Let yer breakfast settle some," she said over her shoulder. "Den take a tablespoon from dat jar in the frig every couple hours. It'll settle dat cough."

"Wait, Nessie," Erin said. "Dhari, would you mind if I looked around? There may be things of historical value that I would buy from you. Nessie may be able to tell me the history behind them."

"Sure. I don't mind at all. Would that be all right with you, Nessie?"

Without a word, Nessie changed direction and headed toward the hall. Erin, towering over the tiny woman, followed her into the dining room.

"So Nessie, you're my tour guide. Give me your Ben Franklin tour of this beautiful old home."

A closed-lipped grin spread the width of Nessie's face. She offered a soft, high-pitched squeak of a laugh.

The request had tickled Nessie's pride and that made Erin smile.

"Dis here's da formal dining room," she said still smiling. "Nobody eats in here 'cept on Sundays and holidays." She passed her hand over the high back of a chair. "I always liked dis room. Makes a person feel special."

"Dis here table and chairs was a gift from the Governor hisself before da war. Miss Anna kept da note to her grandma dat said it was a fittin' gift for a young captain and his wife so's dey could entertain."

Nessie continued around the room, remembering and explaining, then moved to the next. Erin gave Nessie her full attention. She learned about gifts of glassware and furniture bought on a captain's salary, of a bureau and tables bartered with Anna's stitchwork, and broaches and necklace's from Anna's suitors.

"Who is this, Nessie?" Erin stood before an old tintype photo in an ornate frame that hung on the wall.

"Miss Anna's grandma, Adalaine Grayson."

Erin examined the rest of the pictures hanging on the wall of the sitting room, and smaller ones in frames on the tables. "Is there a picture of the captain?"

Nessie frowned. "Oh, no. No pictures of him."

"Is this you?" Erin picked up a framed photo from the table next to the platform rocker. Two teenage girls, one black and one white, wearing flowered dresses and high-top shoes. "And Anna?" They were sitting shoulder to shoulder on the steps of the big porch and smiling sweetly for the camera.

"What we knew den 'bout livin' in dis world." Nessie shook her head.

"If you could, would you want to go back to that time with all your knowledge of living now?"

Nessie pursed her lips and frowned. There was a long silence, then she shook her head again. "Knowin' why, da injustice of da real why, would'a made stayin' behind when Anna went away to school too hard. Tinking da possibilities out dere should be fer me too would'a festered a hurt widout a salve to heal it. Innocence was da beauty of it, da beauty a dem smiles. Can't none of us git dat back."

"I guess not," Erin said, looking again at the smiling faces. "But there is more beauty that I see here—a friendship that thrived in the face of intolerance. Maybe the intolerance made it that much more beautiful."

They heard Dhari begin to cough and turned to find her standing in the doorway.

Erin smiled. "Come and join us. We were just looking at the pictures."

"I heard," she replied with an obvious attempt to keep from coughing. She took the picture Erin handed her.

"Dis one," Nessie added, "is with her grandma jus' before Miss Anna left for nursing school."

"Was she a nurse here in Atlanta?" Dhari asked.

Nessie nodded. "Took care of da children." She pulled a handmade doll from a wicker basket beneath the table. "Long as she could sew, not one little one left da hospital without one o' Miss Anna's dolls." Nessie fluffed the long dress and smoothed the doll's flaxen hair. "Took care o' dem body and soul."

Erin accepted the doll from Nessie. "I can't imagine the patience this must have taken. Look at these tiny stitches, Dhari, the way they sculpt the features on the face and the hands."

Dhari agreed, "It's beautiful work."

"My own abilities in the sewing department," admitted Erin, "don't go beyond Stitch-Witchery and replacing buttons."

Dhari smiled and returned the doll to its basket. "My aunt never had any children of her own?"

"Stayed here, helped take care of her grandma and my momma. Oh, dere was plenty o' suitors over da years, but Miss Anna never saw much use for 'em, 'cept for cuttin' wood and patchin' da roof now and again."

Nessie stood next to the rocker, the back of which was taller than she, and gently fingered the Mikado Lace crocheted piece covering the arm. "I was most the company she had out here after her grandma passed, me and my girls."

Dhari looked into Nessie's eyes as she raised her head. "Nessie, I hope you can forgive me for being so thoughtless. There are things here that mean a lot to you, more than they would mean to me even if I had known my aunt. I want you to have everything of hers you would like."

Nessie splayed a bony hand over her chest. "I keeps all Miss Anna's special gifts right here. Don't need nothin' more."

"They'll be gone otherwise, Nessie, to people who didn't even know her." Dhari let her hand rest atop the old woman's on the arm of the chair. "Think about it, okay? And you don't have to tell me, just take home whatever you know my aunt would want you to have."

"You feel better now," Nessie said, moving toward the hall-way. "You look around, get to know Miss Anna."

"I wrapped leftovers for you. Can I carry them back to your house?"

Nessie shook her head and continued walking.

"There are so many questions I have," Erin called. "Can I come again to visit you?"

"Sure, you come," she said, disappearing down the hall.

"I should probably go, too," Erin said, "and give you a chance to look around and make some decisions on your own."

"No, stay—if you can, that is. There are really no decisions to be made, except for you to tell me what things you'd be interested in if Nessie doesn't want them. Getting sick wasted my vacation days, days that I maybe could have satisfied my curiosity or convinced Nessie that I want her to have my aunt's things. I just don't have any more time to devote to this."

"Well, if not for yourself, then do me a favor? Box up personal papers and pictures and set them aside so that you can go through them when you have more time."

"You don't give up, do you?"

"You have an opportunity that may not be here long to learn so much more than papers and pictures can tell you—a living witness to your family. You are going to regret that decision."

"I won't regret what I don't know. And I shouldn't have to defend myself," she retorted. "My life is complicated enough. My energies are fully extended and I'm overwhelmed. There doesn't seem to be any resolution any where in my life right now, and this situation is the only part that I can pack up and resolve. In order to maintain my own sanity, that's what I have to do."

"I just can't stand to see a chance like this thrown away. I was adopted and I've never been given the opportunity to know where I came from."

"Then you'll never be able to understand why I don't need to know."

53

"No, I guess not," Erin said starting for the door. "I'll put together my recommendations and give them to Terri Sandler."

Before Dhari had time to figure out a response that might restore their earlier congeniality, Dr. Hughes was halfway down the driveway.

An old feeling made an uncomfortable appearance. She was back in high school, when words had too often dropped like gumballs from head to mouth, wondering why she could never say anything right.

Chapter 10

It was only midweek, yet Erin was fighting to keep her eyes open all the way home. The six o'clock sun slipped between the visors of the truck making her squint through her sunglasses. It felt like the fourteenth hour of a twelve-hour day and she couldn't say why. Lectures had gone well, student response was better than average; there had even been time for lunch with a colleague. But, throughout the day her mind had played bigamy with her thoughts. All the while she dressed and drove and lectured, even when she told herself to concentrate, her mind was busily analyzing Dhari Weston.

Erin dressed before the mirror this morning wondering what appealed to Dhari Weston. She lectured today as if Dhari were taking notes, nearly missed her exit trying to pinpoint if there was anything that she could actually like about a person so different than herself. And now, as she thought about it, she realized how much that difference bothered her.

How can she not want to know where she came from? To know her origin? Wasn't she aware of research, of modern thought that gives so much credence to genes over environment in our personal destinies? She was clearly unaware of her privilege. To throw away the right to learn everything you can about your family, especially those who share the same genes, is irresponsible, if not sinful. It shouts of a character flaw so huge I can't believe I'm wasting thought on it.

Erin shook her head, parked her truck in its usual spot in the drive behind her dad's car, and collected her things.

"Dad, I'm home," she called, dropping her keys on the kitchen counter. "Where are you?"

"Out here, Erin."

She continued through the kitchen and the tiny dining area to the open sliding door to the deck. Jacob Hughes was adding an armload of firewood to a knee-high stack beside the door.

"They'll deliver it," he said, short of breath, "but they want another forty bucks to stack it."

"Well, you can save the forty bucks and get the taxpayers to foot the bill for your trip to the hospital, or you can let your daughter stack it, and hang around for a few more years."

She pointed to a chair and continued down the steps to the pile of wood. "Or, you could just let me turn the furnace up on chilly nights and skip this nonsense."

"There's no warmth like a good fire," he remarked from his seat. "Warms you right now, you know? Your mother always loved my fires."

Erin carried her armful to the stack. "Yes, she did."

"That's enough wood for now, Angel. I'll do a little bit each day. Gotta have something to keep this old man going."

"Uh, huh. Did you make that doctor's appointment yet? How long has it been, anyway?"

"Guess I've had my fill of 'em."

"The last one I remember was a while before Mom died."

"What's he gonna tell me? Jake, you're old. You're wearing out? Can't see where doctors did much for your mother."

Silently, she agreed with him. Drugs had only put her mother's multiple sclerosis into remission twice over the years. Her father had probably done more for her quality of life than any of her doctors. He'd lowered the kitchen and bathroom counters, put in a special stove, and widened the doorways to accommodate her motorized chair. He understood how for her to remain vital she had to be useful, needed. The more she needed help from others, the more useful she needed to be to them. She cooked and cleaned as long as she could. She cross-stitched gifts, and became proficient on the computer. He made sure that she got to every committee meeting, and to choir practice, and to every home high school and college basketball game that Erin ever played. Living was her drug of choice and Jake monitored it like a pro.

"I still wish you'd make an appointment. It won't hurt to know that your ticker is ticking normally and that your blood pressure is good." She brought up a few more pieces of wood to even the top of the pile. "I've been better about regular checkups in the last couple of years. I don't know what my genes have in store for me."

Predictably, he changed the subject. "Thank you, Angel, for stacking that up so nice. I've got the best daughter a man could have." He patted the chair next to his and Erin sat down. "You know, I wish your mom could have heard you lecture. She was always so proud of you. She would have loved that."

"I'm glad you finally came to one. When do you want to come to another? I'll tell you what they're about and you pick what interests you."

"Okay, sure. I get a kick out of seeing you up there, teaching all those college kids. I learn a lot, too. But, you know, it would mean even more if I could see your mom watch you." His eyes were noticeably tearing. "Your mom always said that God—"

"Snipped my wings at birth and sent her down an angel."

He smiled and nodded and wiped his eyes unashamedly.

"There have been so many times in my life," she said, taking his hand, "that I've fallen way short of that."

"Never in her eyes, or in mine," he said with a kiss to her cheek. "You'll always be our angel."

~~~~~~~

Like so many other times she would let the conversation end there, with compliment and comfort. No inquiry, no challenge. Not because she wanted it to end that way, but because he needed it to. They'd have dinner; watch a ball game. Things would go on as they always had. Nothing would change, she'd learn nothing about where she came from, until she found the boundaries of his comfort zone and learned to work within them.

She had found her mother's boundaries early. As a teenager she had asked the expected questions: Where are my real parents? Why didn't they want to keep me? The answers were less than adequate: We don't know where they are. We don't know what happened, only that as much as they loved you they just couldn't take care of you.

But it wasn't what the answers didn't tell her that made such an impact on her that day; it was the look in her mother's eyes. She couldn't identify what it was then, but the feeling it gave her was unforgettable. She had decided right at that moment that she would never again be the cause of that look. Whatever she needed to know, she would find out in some other way.

It wasn't until she was an adult that Erin was able to recognize what her mother was feeling. It was partly fear. What if Erin had found one or both biological parents, learned to love them, wanted to be with them? Would she lose the child she loved so much? And partly an undeniable hurt. Didn't her daughter know how much she was loved and wanted? How her heart would ache, how her life would echo, if she ever lost her?

It had been the right decision. Real love would never allow pain when it could be avoided. Now it was up to her father. Doors that she had found locked, he alone would have to open.

Chapter 11

"I'm beginning to think we've got a long distance thing going here," Jamie said as she dropped her jacket on the arm of the couch and joined Dhari at the small dinette table. "You don't have to leave again do you? They can fax you the papers or UPS them or something when it sells, can't they?"

A box the size of a milk crate took up one chair, much of its contents in spilling piles covering the table. Dhari's tone was apologetic. "I didn't get anything done, I was so sick. I brought these papers home because it was all I could do. I have to decide what to do with the contents of the house. There are a few things—"

"Ah, come on, Dhari. You're not going back? This is getting old. I thought you didn't care about anything except selling the place."

"I don't, not really. It's just that," she rose, quickly cleared a spot on the table and turned toward the kitchen, "there's this old woman, Nessie Tinker—"

"Nessie Tinker? Oh, my God!" Jamie added a hearty laugh. "Oh, Dhari, I'm sorry. I shouldn't have interrupted, but that name. It's got to be straight out of the hills."

She felt oddly annoyed at the reference, but dismissed it and placed a cup of coffee in the spot she had cleared in front of Jamie. "She lives on the property adjacent to the Grayson, to my, property."

Jamie stopped smiling long enough to sip her coffee.

Dhari began searching through the piles. "I found something," she said, pulling a paper clear. "Look. It's a sale agreement, dated 1865. My aunt's grandmother, Adalaine Grayson sold fifty acres of land to Charles Jameson, a freed man, for—and get this—'back wages for work on the land'."

Jamie's face had softened into expressionlessness. "I imagine he earned it."

"You imagine and I imagine, because it's 2004. Don't you think it's kind of remarkable for a white landowner in the 1800's to imagine it?"

"Yeah," Jamie shrugged, "I guess."

"Anyway, Nessie's family lived there all those years. Her family was close to my aunt's. At first I thought she worked for my aunt, but they grew up together; they were friends. So, I want to make sure she gets some of my aunt's things; I don't think she'll take them on her own."

"So, one more trip."

"Yeah, that should do it."

"You think you can pull yourself away from," Jamie swept her hand over the table, "all this long enough to go to the Aút Bar? Have dinner, shoot a little pool?"

Dhari brightened. "Sure." She began straightening the piles of papers but Jamie placed her hands on top of them. "Okay, I know," Dhari raised her hands, "too anal. I'll get changed. Be right out."

Despite the fact that she had a more than slight aversion to bars—the smell, the smoke, the drinking too much—Dhari liked the Aút Bar. It was uniquely housed in an old two-story house nestled among other old houses that had been converted into businesses on the north side of Ann Arbor. This old section of town with its farmers' market and resale shops and brick streets was a favorite even before Jamie brought her here to Zingerman's on their first date. It gave off a settled feeling, a feeling of sameness and comfort that reminded her of early childhood in Indiana before all the changes started happening.

Big changes are tough on normal families, but uprooting the Weston family was tumultuous. Leaving friends and neighbors and the few relatives there were, familiar streets and teachers and an external structure that supported struggling self-confidence would be a difficult transition even for the most capable.

What would have happened if Dad hadn't taken the job in Michigan, if we hadn't moved? Would Mom have gotten better instead of worse? Would anything have made any difference? The questions had haunted her for years, but there was no way of knowing the answers, and thinking about it now wouldn't change anything.

She followed Jamie to a little table near the front window overlooking the courtyard, and put it out of her mind. It's just nice to be home, she thought, and leaned over to kiss Jamie on the cheek.

The waitperson leaned across the table to place menus in front of them and Jamie motioned toward Dhari. "Did you see her make a pass at me?"

"Don't be a fool, sweetie," he said with a coy tilt of his head, "order something light and get her home."

Jamie burst into laughter, a sonorous sound that bounded across the room, lifting the heads and putting smiles on the faces of the other patrons.

Dhari, too, smiled. It was how most people reacted to Jamie's laugh—a happy sound that just naturally made others feel good. It was one of the things that first attracted Dhari to her. She had a way of making almost any situation fun. The downside, if you could call it that, was having to share her with so many others. It seemed that everyone wanted to be a part of Jamie's life. Tonight though, Dhari mused, it's just you and me.

And it was just the two of them, eating wet burritos and teasing and laughing. It was therapeutic, her time with Jamie.

She absorbed her confidence, felt protected and safe. Decisions were easy. Jamie didn't mind making them and there was rarely a reason to challenge them. A relationship with little stress—a welcomed sanctuary from the environment she had grown up in, where decisions either weren't made by those who should make them, or met with an unbearable resistance that rendered them useless.

Also on her list of haunting questions was what she would have been like had she grown up in a normal family. Would she have been less fearful and self-doubting? Would she have been more of a leader and less of a follower? Would she have been more like Jamie?

But what tormented her most was the thought that who a person is may be so set in their genes that all the wondering and self-analysis in the world wouldn't alter it one bit. That was the thought that kept her searching for hope for her mother, because altering her mother's fate just might be the key to her own.

Her mind hadn't been on the pool game since she had broken to start it. Jamie, with little need to warm-up, was sinking shot after shot to leave Dhari with a table full of stripes and the impossible task of catching up.

Jamie leaned close as Dhari sighted down the cue stick. "Come on, Minnesota," she whispered. "Let's see something."

"I hate these long ones."

"Stay low on the cue ball and you won't scratch. You should be in good shape for the ten ball here in the side pocket for your next shot."

Dhari looked the table over again. Jamie was right, of course.

"Don't weenie out now, shoot it with confidence."

Dhari sighted again, stroked the stick smoothly through the bridge of her finger and sent the purple stripe sharply into the corner pocket. The cue ball settled with only a slight angle from the ten ball. She tapped it gently into the side pocket, leaving the cue ball near the center of the table. But then, she misjudged the angle of the nine ball to the other side pocket and it bounced off the edge of the bumper. Her best chance to cut Jamie's lead was over and so, Dhari assumed, was the game.

Jamie's shot at the eightball was a long one. It would have to bank off the bumper at the far end of the table and with the correct angle come back to the corner pocket at the close end. Not an easy shot, but one she had seen Jamie make on a regular basis. Dhari's consolation, as the eightball followed a perfect path to the pocket, was that Jamie would be breaking for the next game. Since the bar wasn't crowded yet she would get at least one more game in before others, more capable than she, would be challenging the table.

But before she could get even one shot in the new game the hope Dhari had kept to herself, that Jamie would want to leave early tonight, evaporated as soon as three of Jamie's friends bound noisily up the stairs.

"Que pasa, mi amigos!" shouted Rosie, Dhari's least favorite of the group. "Consider yourselves challenged and about to be beaten. Danny and I are taking you on."

Dhari forced a smile, noted that Sue was once again without a date, and decided to go ahead with her shot. She hoped it would be inconspicuous while Jamie kept their attention. The shot was hurried and the green stripe that should have dropped easily into the corner pocket missed.

"It's a damn good thing you're a better shortstop than you are a pool player," Rosie quipped. "I'll tell you what, you meet me here tomorrow night and I'll give you private lessons."

Danny turned quickly to beat any response from Jamie. "Yeah, that would be the night you turn suddenly single."

"Oh, you don't have to worry. Dhari's a good girl. Right Dhari?"

In this case a perfect angel, Dhari thought with a grin.

Danny shook her head and gave up.

"Have another beer, Rosie," Danny said, claiming an empty stool near the wall. "Come on, you two, get this game over with. I'll be sitting here all night waiting for a challenge."

Dhari swept her hand over the table and gathered the last of the balls to the end of the table. She picked up the rack and began arranging the balls for a new game. "Jamie, you and Danny take this one, I'll sit it out."

"Hey, Babe," Jamie replied, "you didn't have to do that."

"That's all right, I've played enough. I don't mind." I really don't. You play—I'll watch—and everyone will be happy.

Two games later with the upstairs now bustling with activity, the outside challenges began. With Jamie's competitive nature, Dhari knew there would be no thought of leaving until they lost the table. She stood and watched until a stool became available. The conversation with Danny and Sue revolved around the challenges and the shots, and was diced with put-downs and raucous laughter. Once again she was sharing her lover with friends and strangers; sharing Jamie's athletic skills, her social skills, and her time. The occasional winks between shots were little consolation for the loss of an evening that began as time just for the two of them. Not only was it not the first time, she knew it wouldn't be the last.

Dhari spent the rest of the evening watching Sue watch Jamie and fighting comparisons with her mother's paranoia. Complicating matters was the fact that she found it hard to dislike Sue. She was too much like herself—starving for validation, thrilled when it came from someone like Jamie Bridgewater. She studied Sue like she studied an opposing batter—looking for the little signs that would give a shortstop that one step advantage. An early turn of the hips just before a bunt, a drop of the shoulder for a swing and miss to cover a steal. They were subtle, but they were there. When Jamie shot from their end of the table Sue moved her knees only after there was contact; her smiles began and ended with Jamie's attention. She avoided eye contact with Dhari. All indicators of an interest Dhari didn't care to see, but couldn't stop noticing.

Nor did she miss how Jamie responded. Eye contact with Sue lasted longer than was needed, and just now a look only

64

to Sue after a remarkable shot to bank in the eightball. She didn't like what she was feeling, that sense of being excluded, of shared intimacy. Was this really happening right before her eyes? Or was it shades of paranoia? Would Jamie break the only promise they had made to each other, to be honest above all else? Would she sleep with Sue and not tell her? Had she already? Their relationship had weathered dates with others and Jamie's two one-nighters, but it wouldn't survive deception.

Jamie, waiting her turn, took Sue's drink from her hand and helped herself to a sip. Seemingly undaunted by Dhari's stare she sent her a wink and returned the glass to Sue.

Dhari dropped her eyes to the drink in her own hand. So how long do I wait before I ask her? I can't allow angst to jump to anger.

"I can't believe we lost like that." Jamie fastened her seat-belt, but hesitated to start the car. "She puts two balls in on the break then sinks the eightball." She started the engine and backed out of the space without looking at Dhari. "Unbelievable."

"If it were me," Dhari offered, "I'd be thinking that at least they didn't outsmart us or out-skill us; we beat ourselves."

"Not me. No, I'd rather think they had to play the game of their lives to beat us."

"And that would have been the case, I'm sure, if you'd been playing alone. Rosie and her beer are not variables you can control."

"Yeah, I know. That's the sacrifice I make," she said with a sardonic grin, "in order to keep a fresh cache of chides and stories. Rosie, you must admit, is a treasure chest of them."

"She certainly is that. Besides, I could see you getting way too competitive and serious otherwise." She gave Jamie a sideward glance to see if she caught the sarcasm. She hadn't, so she opted for the obvious. "I'm grateful to that cache for keeping me laughing."

"Hey, I'm glad I keep myself laughing. It's a helluva lot cheaper than therapy."

Exactly. "Growing up the lesbian daughter of a Baptist preacher is not all it's cracked up to be, huh?" Dhari said with a smile.

"I'd be peachy if only I'd stop practicing witchcraft and converting young girls into a life of sin," she pulled to a stop at an intersection, waited her turn and accelerated through, "in the church basement."

Dhari grinned and shook her head. "Is that what he thinks?"

"I've gone out of my way to convince him. I applied to teach a Sunday school class for junior high girls. When I was rejected I made up brochures offering séances conducted by Jamica Bridgewater and kept placing them on all the tables and bulletin boards in the church."

Dhari began to laugh.

"I can't believe he can ban a sinner in such obvious need of redemption from the church," Jamie continued. "Isn't that sort of a dereliction of duty?"

"Absolutely," Dhari managed.

"He left me no choice; I had to remind him of his obligation to his ministry."

"I probably shouldn't be encouraging you by thinking this is funny, but I can't help myself." She slapped Jamie's thigh. "So stop laughing to yourself and tell me what you did."

"Oh, but you can't see his face like I still can. You really should have a picture of that in your head to truly appreciate the beauty of it."

Another slap to the thigh. "Come on."

"I had to be there that Sunday. The church was full; the college students were back. He was up there all puffed and pious; the outreach program had produced a record number of baptism requests. He gave his most fervent baptismal talk and disappeared behind the curtain. I almost lost it right then waiting for him to change into his robe. Finally, when I thought I couldn't last another minute, they pulled back the curtain. There he was, in that big stainless steel tub, waiting for the first—" she began to laugh, pulled into a space in Dhari's parking lot and shut off the engine before she could regain her composure. "He had his hands out, waiting for the first convert, and here comes the biggest drag queen you ever saw stepping down into that tub. I lost it. His face said it all. He was disgusted and outraged, and he had to be in that same water and put his hands on this abomination and lay him back in the water."

Dhari laughed hard with her until she finally managed to say, "He couldn't refuse to do it."

"Oh, no, he couldn't. I had him all right. And, it got better; there were three more in the back waiting their turns. He hasn't spoken to me since."

They laughed together until tears spilled from their eyes, and their laughter finally died to giggles. "Aren't you afraid," Dhari asked, "when you do things like that that you'll be looking for a new job the next day?"

Jamie wiped her eyes and shook her head. "Everyone has to have insurance. And as long as I give them the best quote in town, they don't care who I'm sleeping with—even church people have a dollar sign on the bottom line. Don't worry," she said with a wink, "what we do tonight won't make the church bulletin."

"What are we going to do tonight?"

Jamie leaned toward her and gently grasped Dhari's head. She pulled her into a kiss that immediately sent a rush of heat through Dhari's body. All thoughts of Sue had long vanished.

"I'm going to try," Jamie whispered as their lips parted, "to make up for neglecting you all evening."

Chapter 12

The afternoons were still pleasant, untelling of the summer heat to come. Nessie sat on the old wooden bench beneath the giant beech tree that had for all its years provided refuge during the hot and humid months. She smoothed the skirt of her blue cotton dress and spoke to no one beside her.

"Came here late today, but you don't worry none. You know I'll come here 'til da day I pass o're. I'm meetin' her here in just a bit, da one I told ya about with the kind eyes and da weight on her heart. She got secrets she wants knowing, but she ain't ready for dis secret yet. Dhari neder. She got some searchin' to do." Nessie placed her hand against her chest. "Deep in here searchin'... Dere times I ain't got your patience, Anna."

She rested against the back of the weatherworn bench and looked up through the massive branches. In a week, when the leaves are full, she'd no longer be able to see the blue of the sky shining through. "I miss our time here 'neath dis ole tree... I'll read ya more of da book I started yesterday." She opened the book at the marker and began with the poem, *Now Long Ago*.

~~~~~~~

Nessie placed her hand on the page and nodded her head. "Yes," she said aloud, "Dis one's gonna be my favorite." She read the poem again, silently this time, and nodded again. "It surely is. 'Except when silence turns da key into my midnight bedroom and comes to sleep upon your pillow'"

She turned the page, adjusted her glasses and began a new poem. Her reading, though, was aborted at the sound of Erin's truck nearing the top of the drive. "See how anxious she is, Anna? So early, so many questions she has...we'll read again tomorrow," she said, closing the book on her lap and watching Erin approach from the drive.

"What a beautiful day, Nessie," Erin said. "Thank you for allowing me to visit. Here," she said, handing Nessie a foil-covered plate. "I made mincemeat filled cookies. They're my father's favorite dessert. I hope you like them."

"Used to do lots o' baking when da children were home, and the grandchildren. Lost both my girls—one in a car accident, one to cancer. Don't bake no more. I let the grand-children and dere kids do da cookin' now when dere here." She opened the foil and offered the plate to Erin.

"We'll try them together," Erin said with a smile.

Nessie placed her book between them on the bench and started to set the plate on top of it. Erin stopped her momen-tarily to recognize the book.

"Maya Angelou," She said before the plate touched down. "I've read two of her books. I didn't know she had written a book of poems."

"Carletta, my granddaughter, brings me books each week. She loves Ms. Angelou. Makes me read 'em all."

"Carletta is the one who lives in Atlanta?"

"Teachers are good at remembering names."

"I was much better at it when I taught high school, now I don't know my students very well. Too many of them. What does Carletta do?"

"She's an EMT. Anyone who gets sick or hurt, I'd want my Carletta takin' care of 'em." Nessie reached into the pocket of her dress and retrieved a small cell phone. "She got dis for me, pays da bill. Makes me carry it everywhere." She leaned closer and lowered her voice to a whisper. "Even in da ladies room."

"Especially in the ladies room," Erin returned softly. "I've even fallen; I thought I broke my leg. It was such a helpless feeling. She worries about you."

Nessie returned the phone safely and nodded.

"Does she ever try to convince you to move into an apartment in the city?"

"Asked Ms. Anna, too. She said if we sold our places here we could afford a nice new apartment right in her building. She said she's alone and could use da company, but I know she's too busy to be lonely."

"Does she understand why you won't leave here?"

"Maybe some. She has to get past da worry she has for me to get to what feeds dis ole soul. Den she won't want to starve me." Nessie looked directly into Erin's eyes. "You know, don't you?"

"Some days I think I have it all figured out—some days I'm completely lost. I think it has to do with feeling grounded, knowing where you fit into the larger scheme of things. You're a part of this land and its history as much as it is a part of you. Change is unsettling, and scary."

"Change'll come. It always does. Don't see no need to rush it. I like it right here jus fine. Besides, some tings need tellin' first."

Erin nodded and finished her cookie. "How are they?" she asked. "I followed Mom's recipe to the letter."

"Good, good," she said, brushing crumbs from her dress. "Taste real good."

"Nessie, there are so many things I want to know. But if I ask something that's too personal, you tell me, okay? I'll understand."

"You wanna know about the ghost stories."

"Well, yes. There are still a few of those out there. My dad has lived around this area all his life and he's heard them for years."

"Some say Nessie Tinker's a ghost," Nessie said with a tilt of her head. She took Erin's hand and clasped it between her own. "Too warm for a ghost."

"And way too spunky. So, are the other stories similarly unfounded?"

"All depends on what ya believe."

Erin shrugged. "Try me."

"When me an' Miss Anna was girls, before her grandma passed over, dere was dis doll named Billy. It was dressed in a Union uniform and grandma Addy wouldn't let us play wid it. For a while she kept it on a bookshelf, too high for us to reach. An' every day da doll's hat would be on da floor. But we swore we didn't sneak and play wid it, cause we couldn't reach. So, Miss Anna's momma put it high up in da wardrobe closet in her bedroom an' kept da door latched. We was curious, so we would peek in da room on da days when her momma couldn't get outta bed. An' sure as Sherman marched dat Billy's hat would be on da floor an' da door still shut tight. We'd go runnin' down da stairs, out da back door, and hide behind dis big tree an' whisper about ghosts."

"And pretty soon people were talking about how nobody could keep a hat on in the house because the ghost would knock it off."

Nessie offered a squeaky giggle.

"You know I ask these questions partly out of curiosity and partly because Dhari Weston wants to sell this place. I didn't want to have to tell her that she'd be trying to sell a house that locals think is haunted."

Nessie just smiled and shrugged her shoulders.

"You said Anna's momma couldn't get out of bed sometimes, was she sick?"

"Not da kind o' sick dat took to docterin', not back den. Grandma Addy said Ms. Mary jus' couldn't see much good in dis world. Said she couldn't see how pretty blue da sky was an' how sweet da new day smelled after it rained all night. Grandma Addy would lift up our chins like dis," Nessie cupped her hands under Erin's chin, "an' look in our faces and say 'she don't always see da blessing' o' God shinin' in dose faces'."

"Depression."

Nessie nodded.

"Did she ever get better?"

"Not in dis world. Grandma Addy told us Ms. Mary heard how good God's world in heaven was, so she decided to go dere and live. We didn't know no difference dan to be happy dat she got to go some place so good. When we was old enough my momma told us dat she shot herself."

"That must have been hard on you girls."

"Some. Hardest on Emily, Anna's sister. She never was close to my momma; never let Grandma Addy take her momma's place. She and some boy from da feed store left outta here b'fore she was sixteen." Nessie continued looking out across the overgrown field. "Harder times for me and Anna was when Grandma Addy passed o'er, an' my momma." She hesitated and looked again at Erin. Her eyes began to water. "S'pose Miss Anna can see 'em now, can talk to 'em jus' like we used to?"

"Yes," Erin replied, "I'm sure she can."

Nessie looked away again and Erin added, "Hey, would you mind if we have another cookie together? All this talking has made me hungry."

Nessie smiled and took the cookie Erin offered. "Dese do taste good."

"Tell me about this tree, Nessie. I've never seen anything so incredible."

"Older dan me," she squeaked a laugh.

"Easily older than you and me together."

"My great grandpa planted dis o' beech when Miss Anna's family first built dis house." She looked at the massive trunk and pointed to a huge knot. "Lightning took dat big branch dere, jus' da corner o' da roof went wid it. Seen a lot o' good, dis o' tree. Children playin' in her, people eatin' an' gatherin' an' lovin' neath her. Seen da bad, too."

"It survived the fire of Sherman's March, like the house."

Nessie nodded. "My grandma told me dey could see da smoke, smell it day and night, right o'er dat ridge. Can't see da house from dere. Dey all hid in da root cellar, my family and Miss Anna's, afraid to run, afraid to stay. But da fire took da field an' kept comin'. Grandma said dey saw da flames hit da top o' da ridge in da middle o' da night and dey got too scared an' left the cellar an' started runnin' to da woods. When da sun come up my family's little houses was all gone. But, da fire was smolderin' at da path an' da big house was still standin'. Dat's where dey all lived 'til new houses could be built."

"I can't imagine what that would have been like."

"Dat ain't da worse dis o' tree's seen."

Erin frowned and waited for Nessie to continue.

"Gatherin's 'neath here wasn't jus' for weddin's and celebratin' and happy times. Dere was mournin' for da passed, an'," she pointed to a large limb about ten feet up and parallel to the ground, "dere it bore my Rufus."

It took only a second for Erin to realize what Nessie meant. She took the old woman's hand. "Oh, Nessie, I'm sorry. You don't have to tell me any more if you'd rather not."

"He never did no harm to nobody but hisself. Didn't do no good for no one neither, 'cept he gimmie my two girls. But dere weren't no reason for him to die like dat."

"And no one was punished for it, right?"

"Dere was no way o' knowin' back den, dere was so many. Da punishment was for Miss Anna, for her family lovin' dere niggers."

Erin squeezed the hand she still held.

"Dere was no man in Miss Anna's house, else he'd been hangin' right dere next to my Rufus."

"For not protecting his women, or not keeping their attitudes in line. We come from a confused lot, white southerners. Women had to be strong enough and smart enough to raise the children, teach them to read and teach them their religion, and even manage the help. But, that airy, southern belle image had to be kept alive so that there was something so helpless and vulnerable that all the chivalry and killing was justified. Change is uncomfortable and slow," she squeezed the old lady's hand again before releasing it, "but we're getting there, Nessie. I truly believe we're getting there."

"But ya can't know where ya are now 'less ya know where ya come from. My girls knew, an' my grandchildren know—told 'em right here under dis tree." Nessie patted the palm of her hand against her chest. "What dey know in here is what dey gonna see in dis world. Pride will seek out da proud—love will find da loving."

"Amen, Nessie Tinker, amen."

Chapter 13

Erin stopped momentarily in the hallway of Terri Sandler's home to admire the photographs on the wall. The most beautiful buildings of Atlanta's nightscape: the Peachtree Towers with twin tops of illuminated columns, the lighted pyramid atop the Sun Trust Plaza, the cylindrical light and antenna of the Westin Peachtree, the Bank of America with its see-through pyramid of light. Each picture professionally matted and framed.

Surely, this is one of the country's most unique and attractive cities at night, and I'll bet Dhari Weston has never seen it this way. How could she? She was following strange directions, worried about missing a turn, trying to keep up with traffic, to say nothing of her obvious time constraints. Maybe I could show it to her, take her thoughts to fun places where whatever it is that locks her in constant stress can't intrude. Maybe I can find something that will soothe away the angst on her face. I wonder what Dhari Weston looks like when she smiles.

"Beautiful aren't they?" Terri said from behind her.

"Yes," she said with a quick turn of her head. "Sometimes I forget how beautiful Atlanta is."

"Joyce took those. They turned out so well I had them framed for her. It made her smile like a little girl whose mother just taped her latest creation to the front of the refrigerator. I'll do anything for that smile."

Joyce's voice interrupted them from the dining room, "Hey, you two, I didn't spend hours on this dinner so it can get cold."

Terri took Erin's arm. "Come on, that's one Italian we don't want to insult."

"Absolutely not," Erin replied.

The meal was classic Joyce: escarole soup, cold antipasto, veal piccata, and rigatoni. Delicious, and to Erin's palette, Italian perfection. There had been evenings when she left here swearing that she wouldn't be able to eat again for a week. And as guilty as it made her feel to have eaten so many meals here and have not returned the favor, she knew better than to turn down an invitation. Joyce loved to cook, loved entertaining company, and just as obviously loved Terri.

Erin watched as Joyce ran her hand over the side of Terri's head and kissed her cheek before she sat down. You don't leave family, friends, and a high-paying job in New York for someone unless you love them. Erin felt good around these two women, she felt comfortable and wanted in their home. And as usual, her contributions tonight, homemade bread and the Grayson property recommendations, seemed small in comparison.

"So, you think she should register the house as a historical site," Terri began.

Erin nodded and finished her last sip of wine. "Keep a few acres around the house for a buffer, get the best price she can on the rest of the land, and sell the house separately. The only problem she might face would be selling property that would be considered of independent historical significance, like a battlefield."

"What's involved in registering the house?"

"The property has to be nominated to the National Register for historic designation. I have no doubt that it'll meet the criteria, but Dhari will have to go through her aunt's papers and collect proof—deeds, transfers, sales, anything with transaction dates and descriptions of the property. Pictures would help as well."

"I'm already doing that for her. I'll take some more interior shots."

"She should have a preservation easement incorporated into her deed and registered with the county. That'll protect the property from future inappropriate alterations, demolition, neglect, and even encroaching development."

Terri had snatched a paper and pen from the cabinet drawer and was busy scratching down notes.

"She'll need special insurance. Terri, don't worry about getting all this, I'll make a copy of everything for you. Just a little reassurance about the insurance and I'll shut up. The National Trust has partnered with two companies, the Chubb Group and MIMS International, to offer coverage for restoration, rebuilding, and replacement costs for antique furnishings. It's a must."

Terri leaned back in her chair and shook her head. "She's gonna freak, absolutely freak."

"Well, there's also a huge advantage. With a preservation easement the property continues on the tax roll at its current standing, a good selling point. It won't be able to be taxed at its 'highest and best use' so that's a tremendous tax break."

"It all makes perfect sense to us and probably a lot of people living in this area. But to Dhari Weston? This is going to be a hard sell."

"But it's the smartest, most conscionable way to go."

"And it keeps her involved with this property way longer than she has any intention. Who's going to convince her it's worth it?"

"You're the realtor," Erin replied with a smirk. "I'm just trading my expert opinion for a fantastic dinner."

Terri offered a quick laugh that stopped short of being convincing. "You'd better give me more ammunition then."

"Why do you think Terri should even try to convince her to go to all that trouble?" Joyce asked. "She wants to get it sold, right? Why not let the new owners register it?"

"Dhari will get the biggest benefit instead of the new own-ers. The land should sell fast enough, don't you think, Terri?"

"Building is still booming. They can't build houses fast enough. That won't take long. It'll just be a matter of getting the best price for her. She'll definitely make more selling them separately."

"Maybe that'll offset having to wait longer to sell the house," Erin added. "And if it's a historical site she may be able to overcome the outward physical condition, and hope-fully downplay the ghost stories."

Terri nodded in agreement, but Joyce waited for eye contact from Erin. "I think there's a third rationale."

Erin returned a questioning look.

"All this is going to buy time and keep Dhari involved, and I think you're hoping she'll eventually change her mind and keep the house."

Terri unleashed a rumble of a laugh. "There's my girl, zoom lens zeroing right in on the essence of it."

The smile Erin returned was not the usual wide and bright, but rather reserved—one that was meant to protect feelings not ready for scrutiny. "I keep thinking that if it were me, I'd keep it—but, I'm not her. It's not fair of me to judge her by what I might want or need in my life."

Terri leaned forward and studied Erin carefully. "You don't think it has anything to do with big brown eyes and a tight little body tugging at that unmentionable part of you?"

"You know, just because I'm single doesn't mean that everything in my life revolves around getting laid."

"Yeah, I'm not so sure about this one," Terri replied. "This is going way past your normal dinner fee. You're spending an awful lot of time on—"

"A project that is directly related to my teaching."

"Bullshit," Joyce chortled, refilling Terri's wine glass. "You're hooked."

"That's funny," Erin returned. "You'd think I would feel a hook that's sunk deep enough in my jaw for you to notice."

"You're manually overriding, like a more sophisticated

camera—you override the automatic setting when you're looking for a different outcome." Joyce was looking right at her, brown eyes wide and serious. "It's an unlikely situation— she's there, you're here—neither of you is likely to move. You're no spaghetti-head, it's a smart thing to override that instinct."

Terri started a quiet rumble that could easily lead to a full-blown laugh if she let it. Joyce looked at her. "I'm right," she said, still serious. "You know I am."

Erin chose to let it drop.

Terri moved her head slowly from side to side. "I'm telling you, Erin, if my girl here could have fifteen minutes with Ms. Weston, she'd have her figured out for us."

"Are we trying to figure her out?" Erin asked.

Terri's smile had softened into contemplation. "Oh, I think she has us both wondering what's behind the angst. It seems as out of place as a three-piece suit and Mickey ears."

"Bring her over," Joyce offered. "As long as she's no *carvone*. You know I won't tolerate a *carvone* in my house, eating my food and burping in my face. There's no amount of angst that'll excuse rudeness." She gathered a handful of empty plates and disappeared into the kitchen.

Carvone, Erin mused. In any language the concept was the same, and thanks to good southern upbringing it was one Erin understood well. She never appeared at another's door empty handed and always left with graciousness and grati-tude. No one needs worry about the social graces of Erin Hughes, but suddenly she had concerns about those of Dhari Weston. How would she stack up to someone else's analysis, to Joyce Fratellini's? To Jake's? And why don't I trust my own analysis?

"What are you thinking so hard about?" Terri asked.

"Nothing really. Just thinking about how much I like Joyce. There's never any guessing about whether she likes you or not, is there?"

"No, ma'am. To some that's a blessing, to other's it's a curse. I, on the other hand, can smile in a client's face the whole time my mind is screaming 'asshole'. Sometimes it bothers Joyce that I can do that."

"Have you found yourself smiling in Dhari Weston's face?"

Terri looked temporarily surprised. "Actually," she replied with a thoughtful expression, "no. I can't tell you exactly what it is, but there is something in her eyes—and if you've noticed she's always looking directly into your eyes, like she's looking for something there—that makes me want to do everything in my power to make things right for her. Do you feel that, too?"

"Yeah, and then I get even more frustrated and start pissin' myself off for trying."

This time Terri let go of a full-blown laugh that alerted Joyce in the kitchen. "Come on, now," she said, reappearing with plates of dessert, "save the fun until I can join you."

Terri's laugh died quickly to a chuckle. "Well, the doctor here is pissin' herself off, so you know we're in for a good story."

"There's no story," Erin insisted. "I just keep making suggestions and getting responses that are totally opposite than I expect. I have to learn to keep my mouth shut and stay out of the personal part of this."

"Exactly what I have to do as a realtor. I try to read people so that I can make appropriate suggestions, but I've found the best thing to do is listen—and to remember that their decisions are based on experiences and needs that I'm not privy to."

"So, what are we deciding here, that we need to stay out of Ms. Weston's personal business and stop trying to figure her out no matter how tempting it is?"

Joyce scowled at Terri's eye contact. "Don't look at me," she said, "I've never met the woman. You meatballs are on your own."

Terri looked at Erin and tipped her head toward Joyce. "She thinks we're going to muddy the lines here and get in over our heads."

"Are we?"

"Not we, doctor. I'm just the realtor."

Chapter 14

Rich Avery tapped an open palm against the outside of Dhari's cubicle before crossing the doorway. It was a gesture his employees appreciated since a personal visit from the Great Lakes AIDS Coalition director was a rare and somewhat privileged occasion.

Dhari turned from her computer screen and started to get up.

"Sit down, sit down," he waved, rolling the cubicle's second chair into position and sitting down. "How's everything going today?"

"Fine, Rich. I'll have the finished app for the Baker Douglas grant ready for approval today. Erik wanted it on his desk tomorrow."

"Oh, I don't doubt it will be ready. I was speaking more in general terms. Erik mentioned you had some family matter to take care of."

Rich Avery had no reputation for asking questions that led you to unwittingly sabotage yourself. But years of living with a mother who so often did, sent an automatic warning of silence that delayed Dhari's response. She searched the softly wrinkled face and direct eyes for a sign that it was safe, but it came in his next words.

"He wasn't specific. I hope everything's all right."

"Yes, things are okay. An aunt passed away," she replied, then quickly responded to his frown. "I've never met her, so it hasn't been an emotional thing. For reasons unknown though, she left everything to me. I was hoping that it would only take one more trip, but nothing is working out as I had planned."

"Things rarely do," he said with a smile. "Life would be much too easy if they did. Someone, I'm assuming the creator of this magnificent universe, decided that we need challenges to our intellect and tolerance. When I was younger I took them on like a pumped up freshman halfback. Now, there are times when I'm ready to forfeit. Enough lessons, just let me have a little monotony, you know?"

Dhari smiled at his candor. "I think I've reached that point already. I wonder what it would be like if we could count on things going our way? To be that free of worry."

"Actually, I saw a movie over the weekend, Margaret got some two-for-one deal at Blockbuster, and it was about that very thing. Can't remember the name of it, Jeff Daniels was in it. Anyway, this whole town saw life in black and white; their existence was black and white. They went to the same places, ate the same foods, experienced the same outcomes day after day."

"Good outcomes?"

"Right. No threats to the status quo. The husband comes home to his favorite meal every night, the most popular girl in school always bakes cookies for the star athlete, the basketball team never loses."

"No disappointments, no failures."

"And no conflict. But when a brother and sister come into town from somewhere else, people begin to realize that the consequence for their ideal existence is a lack of excitement and passion. When conflict is introduced, and uncertainty becomes real, the characters one by one begin to feel challenged. The result? Excitement and passion, shown in the form of color. By the end of the movie the whole town saw their world in full color—the good and the bad."

"The moral being that without threat of failure there can be no glory in achievement."

"Very simplistic, really. We can't experience a real high without ever feeling a real low." He smiled and shook his head. "I told my wife that I thought it was a silly movie. I expected a better venue for Jeff Daniels—he lives just outside of Dexter, you know, not too far from me—but, I've been thinking about that silly movie ever since." He laughed and patted the palms of his hands on the arms of the chair. "My wife's not cooking tonight, she's playing cards with some friends. I guess I'll pick up a sub on the way home."

"Okay, I promise not to complain about a couple of trips down south."

"There you go," he said with a nod of his head. "Which brings me back around to the other reason I'm taking up your time today. Don't use up any more of your vacation days. If you need days during the week, or even a week, to get things taken care of properly, I want you to sign out a company laptop and you and Erik can work through e-mail. I don't care where it gets done, as long as it gets done."

"Thank you, Rich," she said, relief evident on her face. "That's going to relieve an enormous amount of stress for me."

He nodded. "That's my intent, along with giving you some time to think about something. We're going to be losing Eric to a company in California. It gives him an opportunity to go back home where much of his family lives. I asked him for a recommendation from within the company for his replacement. Without hesitation he named you."

"Oh," she exclaimed, unable to think of a more appropriate response.

"Like I said, think about it. I'd like you to apply for it. I'll send you over a full job description. Also, take some time to talk to Erik about it."

"I will," she said as he rose. "Thank you for considering me."

He waved off the thanks. "I know my people pretty well. You're never late, you called in sick once in the past year, and you always meet your deadlines." He started out the door and turned his head to smile at Dhari. "It's appreciated."

She returned the smile. "Have a great day, Rich, and thank you again."

Chapter 15

The morning sun glistened brightly on the remaining mounds of snow lining the sidewalk. Donald Weston removed the Saturday paper from the box at the curb and took a moment to notice the wispy tails of cirrus clouds against a pale blue sky. Spring would be early this year; he could feel it. And close behind it, the summer term, the first one free of classes in many years. He had taught the summer term years past his privilege not to, partly out of habit, partly because he was uncomfortable with the thought of spending that much time at home.

This time, though, when it came time to commit, Dhari's words decided for him. *Find a way to convince her, or you are going to lose the rest of your family.* She was right. He had known it but not owned it for a very long time. And it was days like this that had made that possible.

He placed the paper on the counter as his wife entered the kitchen. "It's a beautiful day for a walk, Sweet Pea," he said, pulling a green jacket from the hook and helping her into it. "You won't need anything heavier than this."

"OK," she said, "but you wear this for me." She stretched up and placed his cap on his head, then patted his cheek. "I've got a little bit more covering my head than you do."

He tugged the cap into place and gave her a wink. "Let's go. There's a marvelous day awaiting us."

They walked for blocks, hand in hand, noting changes in the neighborhood, wondering about old neighbors. It took them back years, remembering their children's playmates, laughing at their childhood antics.

"Do you remember the day Mrs. Campbell called and asked us if we knew the kids had been on the roof?"

"I was so stunned." Lela replied. "I asked her whose kids. She got so huffy. 'Your kids', she said, 'Dhari and Douglas'."

"I'm still amazed that none of the other kids squealed on them. They must've looked forward to the 'game' every time you went grocery shopping." Don shook his head and led them to a dry bench on the elementary school playground. "Let's sit here for a bit in the sun."

"The only thing Dhari wanted for her birthday was that stopwatch. I had no idea what she'd end up doing with it."

"I'll bet you to this day Douglas won't admit that he never beat her time. Out the front bedroom window, across the porch roof, up the rake of the big roof, down the back to the TV tower, down that and around the house and upstairs to the start. Wow, what a game."

"I was furious. I don't know who I was most mad at, Dhari and Douglas, or Donna for not putting a stop to it and telling me. And you weren't much better. A week's allowance," she said with a coy look out of the corner of her eye, "not much of a punishment for something so dangerous."

"If I tell you a secret will you promise not to get mad?"

"How long have you kept this secret?"

"I don't know, two years? A couple of Thanksgivings ago the kids were confessing childhood pranks."

"Where was I?"

"You weren't feeling well."

"I miss a lot, don't I?"

Don put his arm around his wife's shoulders. "Shall I tell you?"

"Will it make me laugh?"

"Can't guarantee it."

"Well, no one's in prison. They're alive and have all their extremities." She leaned her head back against his shoulder. "I guess it can't be too bad."

Don scanned the roofs of the houses across the street from the school. "It's made me look at roofs quite differently." He looked into Lela's uplifted face. "Ours wasn't the only roof they climbed. Dhari challenged Douglas to every roof on our block and Campbell's. But Ellen Campbell didn't know that it was her roof, the highest and steepest, that Dhari scaled and Douglas chickened out on."

"Ignorance is bliss." She said as a soft smile eased across her face. "What do we know about our Dhari?"

"What we didn't know then. That she would have kept climbing roofs, no matter what my punishment, until she found one that Douglas couldn't. Hey," he said with a squeeze of her shoulders, "will you do something for me?"

"What?"

"Smile like that again for me?"

"Oh," she said and pulled away with a slap to his chest.

"Really. I remember when that smile put the sun in its place."

Lela obliged.

"And it still does."

"I don't make it easy for you to stay. I'm sorry for that."

"I'm not teaching the summer term."

"But why? You always teach the summer term."

"I want us to take a vacation."

Lela sat up straight. Her face brightened noticeably. "Where would we go?"

"Wherever you want. How about Hawaii? That was your dream before the kids."

"I'd forgotten about Hawaii."

"Forgotten, or did you give up on it?"

Lela only stared ahead, leaving Don as she so often did to wonder, to piece together as best he could what may be going on in his wife's mind. There had been a time when he could read her, when they talked about dreams and how to make them come true. Once their dreams had been important, and plausible. They had wanted the same things, to bridge the oceans and hike ancient paths, to experience cultures they had only read about. Children, too, were important—maybe not so many quite so soon, but he always thought he and Lela would have their time to find their dreams. He needed to know now if it was too late.

"I was seventeen," Lela was still staring across the playground, "the missionaries were touring the churches with slides of their stay in Hawaii. I had never seen anything so beautiful, and haven't since. The colors were so vivid that I can still see them in my mind."

"We'll go," he said. "We'll see them for real."

"I've never planted flowers because I knew nothing could ever be that beautiful."

"We'll take our own pictures and hang them all over the house when we get home—an inside garden right from paradise."

Lela turned and looked into her husband's eyes. "Do you think I could? Go, I mean."

The look on her face beamed with youth and hope, and stirred in him an excitement that had long been dormant. This was his sweet Lela, his pride, his love, his reason to hope. He hugged her tightly. "Of course you can."

Suddenly, she pushed from his embrace and stood. "I'd just spoil it," she said turning away. "We shouldn't even talk of it."

Not ready to give up, he quickly caught up to her "Let's try a new doctor. There are new medications now."

"Let's not spoil the rest of the day."

Chapter 16

Dhari checked the directions on the paper stuck over the slide control on the dash. Maneuvering her way through the suburbs of Atlanta wasn't as nerve-racking as she thought it would be. Erin's directions were as easy to follow as Terri Sandler's. Maybe it's a southern thing, she mused, such care given to details. Get to your left early so you don't have to cross two lanes of traffic at the last minute—really helped. Go slow past the Suds 'n Duds—street sign hidden by tree branches—yep, right there.

She couldn't believe how at ease she felt. She hadn't gotten lost, or frustrated; she hadn't cursed the Grayson house once. As soon as she could she'd look for a nice thank-you gift for Rich Avery. He was a blessing she hadn't expected. Reminding herself of the blessings in her life was a practice she needed to nurture. Concentrate on the positive—ignore the negative. Good thoughts will keep your mind healthy.

"Three blocks down." Dhari checked the directions again. "Right side. Small taupe house with white trim. Cute. White Ram out front. Thank you, Doctor."

She pulled into the driveway just as Erin appeared at the front door. The jump Dhari's heart took surprised her. Just because a woman looks good in her jeans is no reason to turn the hormones loose, she reminded herself. Purely physical responses are normal, to be expected. They'd been occurring for as far back as she could remember—junior high. No, sixth grade, it was sixth grade when she first felt the heat from just a two-second look into Ms. Stevens's eyes. The dilemma it caused was whether to have Daddy switch her to Ms. Stevens's class where she could see her all day, every day, but where it was doubtful that she could survive a whole day so short of breath and shaking with nervousness. It was a dilemma unsolvable by the naïve mind of a young lesbian. It was a request never made. She merely allowed the heat to let her take every possible opportunity to look into those eyes.

The mature lesbian mind will have no problem managing the heat and the erratic heartbeat Dr. Hughes seemed capable of causing. I'll just enjoy it for what it is, appreciation of a woman who shouldn't look that good.

"Come in for a few minutes," Erin called from the doorway. "I want you to meet my father."

Dhari nodded. She turned off the radio, searched for the door lock and fought a sudden jealousy that she had never been able to invite friends into her home without fear of embarrassment. Even before the teenage 'my-parents-are-so-weird' stage, and after when college friends should have been welcomed home for weekends, Dhari feared the judgment her mother's behavior would bring upon her. Would they think she was crazy, too? Would they feel uncomfortable and avoid her because they wouldn't know what to say? Or, would they tease her, make fun of something she had no control over? She had never been willing to take that chance. And the shame of it, beyond the obvious, was that her father never saw the pride she felt for him because avoiding one almost always meant avoiding them both. It seemed so unfair.

But I'll meet Erin's father and I'll like him and I'll be happy for her, she thought, and greeted Erin with a smile.

"Do you mind?" Erin asked. "He loves to meet new people."

"No. No, not at all. Every parent should have a daughter so proud."

~~~~~~~

Pip, a longhaired Chihuahua mix with a fresh terrier cut, was the first to greet her. Three pounds of black and tan wiggle circled her ankles and sniffed, and even stood tall on her back legs to get a better vantage point as Dhari knelt to pet her. Her assessment made, Pip jumped onto Dhari's lap as soon as she was seated at the dining table, and lavished her with welcoming kisses until Erin told her to stop.

Jake Hughes beamed with a boyish smile throughout the introduction and initial pleasantries. His interest was genuine, his enjoyment obvious. Dhari found herself being unusually open and honest, and answering questions without hesitation. Where was she from, how large her family, did she like sports, who was her favorite author? Anne McCaffery, a southern man who reads McCaffery. Who would've figured?

She did indeed like Jake Hughes. She liked his candor, his inoffensive sense of humor, his smile, and she liked that he seemed to like her.

"You know what I'm bettin'?" Jake said with a wink. "I'm bettin' that the first southern accent you heard here reinforced a pretty negative stereotype." He watched Dhari lower her eyes from his gaze, and reached across the table to touch her arm. "No, now listen. See, now that embarrassed you, which means I'm right about the last hour changin' that attitude—at least some. Am I right? What was the first heavy accent you heard?"

Dhari offered a reluctant look, but complied. "I asked what was on a fast food sandwich. The woman said, 'Well, ya gotch yer ham, ya gotch yer turkey, ya gotch yer pickles. All raght there'."

Erin and Jake both chuckled unashamedly.

"Yeah, she's one of ours," Jake said. "Horse-drawn slow and magnolia sweet. And it's got nothin' to do with how many brain cells are fully operative."

"Why do you think I sound the way I do when I teach?"

Erin asked. "If I wanted to be taken seriously in other parts of the country, I had to lose the accent."

"Was it hard to do?"

"It took concentration. A lot of concentration." She admitted, then added with a full accent, "And yes, darlin', I do slip now and again."

The sound, coming from the mouth of Dr. Hughes, was both strange and appealing. Strange because she knew how smart this woman was, appealing for the same reason. Would she have had the same first impression of the good doctor if that lecture had been in full southern accent?

The jump from preconceived ideas to prejudice was a short one.

"I had no idea," Dhari admitted, "that I was that prejudiced."

Jake had been quiet too long. "Have you ever heard a stupid Brit?" He raised his eyebrows in question. "Not that there aren't any, but it's kinda like a reverse prejudice that makes them all seem brilliant. Even a cockney accent doesn't leave people thinkin' they're as born-in-the-hills stupid as someone with a southern drawl. It seems to be the only accent where you have to live it to respect it."

"I hope you aren't taking any of this as a personal affront, Dhari. I often think Dad missed his calling behind the lectern."

"No," Dhari directed toward Jake, "don't feel bad about opening my eyes."

"Good, good," he returned. "I'm not one to apologize for intelligent conversation."

Erin rose from the table, crossed behind his chair, leaned down and kissed him on the cheek. "No, certainly not." She motioned with her head for Dhari to follow her. "If you want to avoid an obvious, but charming, bit of schmoozing we'd better get out of here."

"Jake, you're not joining us for dinner? I don't mind schmoozing," Dhari said as she rose. "I really don't."

Jake looked at his watch. "No time for that. Georgetown's playing tonight. Every time I don't watch, they lose."

"I might be late, Dad. I'm going to show Dhari around town some after dinner. I'll try not to wake you."

"If I'm still on the couch you'll know what kind of game it was."

"What kind of food do you like, Dhari?"

"I'm not fussy."

Erin snapped in her seatbelt. "Okay, let me put it another way. What is a favorite food that you never seem to get enough of?"

"Well that makes it easier. Barbecue ribs."

"Wet or dry, sweet and hot, I know where they make the best ribs in Atlanta. Some argue they're the best in the south. Good music and good food. We're on our way."

"Is that where you want to go?"

"I happen to love ribs, but it doesn't matter, this is your treat."

Dhari looked sharply at Erin. "You're not paying for this."

Erin took her foot off the accelerator and the truck slowed quickly. "Then we're not going. I told you on the phone that I wanted to apologize for making judgments I have no right to make. This evening is my way of saying I'm sorry."

"It's overkill, Erin. You already apologized. You're making me feel like my apology for being so rude to you isn't enough."

They were stopped at a four-way stop, two cars past their turn to go. Erin waved still another car through ahead of them. "It's your decision, Dhari, either dinner at Fat Matt's Rib Shack, or you're welcome to come home with me and watch the game with Jake. I must warn you though, his idea of game food is kettle-corn and beer."

"Okay, now I see how you work. You get me so up for the taste of ribs that I can't resist. Not that an evening with Jake wouldn't be just fine."

Erin laughed and propelled the Ram through the intersection. "He is a beauty, my dad. A real social animal. He loves to talk and he misses his best friend terribly. I do what I can, but nothing can take the place of Mom for him."

"I'm sorry, Erin."

"Yes, I am too, for a loss we're both suffering. She was an important part of our lives."

This time Dhari was sure, Erin's eyes were tearing. She had turned her head, but not before Dhari had seen. The impending silence was uncomfortable. This was something Dhari had never been good at, knowing when to say something, when to keep quiet. And if saying something would help, would she find the right words? Maybe just honesty? Yes, honesty would have to do.

"I've never lost anyone close to me. I won't pretend to understand how you feel."

"The thing about losing someone," Erin said without taking her eyes from the road, "is that you'd better have peace in your heart about them."

More silence.

"I used to fight embarrassment when I was young...for my parents. They were so much older than other parents. I always had to explain that they weren't my grandparents. I'd get embarrassed, then I'd see them in the bleachers cheering and so proud of me, and I'd hate myself. And there were times when I didn't tell them about a school event..." The truck slowed to a stop at a light. Erin turned to make direct eye contact with Dhari. "One of those times my mother found out, an unexpected conversation with another mother at the drugstore. She asked me about it; I lied and said that I had forgotten. She never brought it up again."

"She probably believed you."

Erin shook her head. "She knew. About that, and my desire to find my biological parents, and more. She didn't miss anything. And I knew it." The light turned, Erin's focus returned to the road. "And I never made it right...even on her death bed; I couldn't make it right."

Dhari felt her throat tighten. It surprised her, along with the emotion that caused her own eyes to water. It was obvious that even with her head turned Erin was wiping tears from her cheeks. All Dhari could think of was that she should tell Erin that it was all right, that surely her mother had known what was in her heart. But she couldn't say what she didn't really know. She blinked back her own tears, and cleared her throat to ease the tightness. *Why can't I say it? Just to make her feel better. What harm would it do? Say it.*

"I'll never be at peace, either," came out instead.

"About your aunt?"

"No, it's a complicated situation. Not the norm by a far stretch."

Erin glanced at Dhari briefly, eyes dry now and contemplative. "There's very little about my life that can be considered normal. Maybe we're not so different after all, you and I." She glanced again and continued. "Maybe the difference between us is how we live our lives around it."

"In spite of it." *God, here we are again, closed in and spilling over in a moving confessional. Eyes devoted ahead— denying intimacy, while laying bare the truth with no one looking in your face for the effects it's had on your soul.*

"Spite wastes too much energy," Erin was saying. "It doesn't change the abnormal to normal, or make the past any different. It tries to produce positive results from negative reactions. 'I'll show the world; I'll be a respected, admired teacher despite the fact that my real parents didn't value me at all.' I think I've come a lot further by believing that I am who I am, and that I am blessed in ways that have allowed me to be who I am. I have been surrounded with love and opportunity, and I have wrapped that around the negatives so tightly that they've been meshed into the fabric of me."

"With or without therapy?"

Erin laughed. "You sound like a friend of mine. She has this way of shifting the grain from the chaff right before your eyes." She nodded at Dhari. "Yes, some therapy, during those breaking away years in college."

"My mother's crazy." *God, I said it.* Dhari took a breath that she intended to be deep and full. It was not. She felt sick

95

to her stomach.

"For all I know, mine may be, too."

"I've never told anyone, not even lovers."

"Partly out of respect for your mother, and partly so that others wouldn't judge you. The same reasons that I didn't tell anyone that I was adopted for the longest time."

"I can't believe I told you."

"It was time. We are creatures of nature, subject to its laws. Anything suppressed in nature eventually finds its way to the surface. I'm just lucky enough to be sitting here when it did."

"Lucky?"

Erin eased the truck into one of the few parking spaces left and turned off the key. "It's an intimacy few get to experience, and I feel honored." Dhari was looking straight into her eyes, but said nothing. "Come on," Erin said with a smile. "Let's continue this conversation around the best ribs you'll ever taste. Then, I'll show you Atlanta at night."

"It is beautiful," Dhari said. "Your city at night. Thank you for taking the time to share it with me."

The Ram was stopped in front of the house, but neither of them had made a move to leave the truck.

"It was part of a plan," Erin admitted. "But as it turned out, it wasn't necessary. The objective was reached early on and the rest of the evening was pure pleasure for me, too."

"This wasn't a date, was it? I'm involved with someone, so I didn't want this to be a date."

"It was an apology," Erin reassured her, "and a tour, an old-fashioned southern tour."

Dhari returned a look that barely hid the effort it was taking her not to smile. "A plan," she said. "Was dinner part of this plan, too?"

"No," Erin replied, holding up a hand. "Dinner was just what I said it was—well, maybe a little more—it includes a promise to stay out of your personal business concerning the house."

"So, the plan?"

"Was to get you to smile. But I hadn't counted on Jake accomplishing that before we even got out the door."

"I didn't realize that I presented such a challenge. I guess I've been pretty self-absorbed over the past month." Over the past few years if I were honest. "So, it showed that much. What an ugly impression I must be leaving."

"No, not ugly. Besides, I've been where you are, not wanting to get to know anyone, not wanting to get attached because I'd have to leave. Year after year it was a new city, a new college, new people. And when you don't get involved, relationships tend to be superficial at best." Erin leaned back against her door. "I will admit, though, that I hoped I'd have time to see beneath that façade of yours." Her smile gleamed in the darkness. "And I have. And I'm glad I did."

Dhari shook her head. "You're embarrassing me and flattering me at the same time. I have been a self-absorbed, unappreciative shithead and I'm sorry. I don't deserve the effort you've made. I'm sure you have better things to do than provide opportunities for me to redeem myself."

"Not really." She nodded toward the house.

Dhari turned to look and in the front window, between the drawn drapes, was a tiny black face and ears the size of small bat wings. "Well, somebody waited up for you."

"She didn't get her walk because Jake undoubtedly fell asleep on the couch. It must not have been a close game."

"Are you going to take her?"

Erin pulled the keys from the ignition. "I have a hard time resisting cute faces and wet kisses."

Dhari smiled at the probable implication. "Can I join you?"

"You don't have to ask."

Pippin stood still just long enough for Erin to attach her leash, then wiggled and danced and stood on her hind legs until Dhari knelt down and fussed over her. "Yes, you are sweet," she said, accepting kisses to her chin. "You are the cutest little thing I think I've ever seen."

Pip circled them both, made sure she had their attention,

then led them off down the sidewalk.

"Those were my mother's words almost exactly," Erin began. "They were perfect for each other. Pip was light enough to be in Mom's lap so she got her undivided attention. And she was smart enough, when Mom's voice got weak, to come and get us when she needed something. Pip was an emotional mess, too, for a long while after Mom died." Erin knelt beside a very alert Pip and unfastened her leash so that she could chase a rabbit through the nearest hedge. "She's out of her funk now. I know I don't take Mom's place, but I think she likes me all right."

Pip pranced back to the sidewalk, her mission accomplished, and Erin let her walk free. "You're sure a hit with her, and my dad. It goes to a theory I have," she continued. "If you want to test your assessment of someone, introduce them to your parents and your dog."

Pip turned her head to assure that both humans were right behind her, and picked up her pace again.

"What if I'm putting on an act? A female Eddie Haskell."

"Well, Eddie wouldn't last ten minutes with Jake. A couple of opinion questions and the 'yes, sirs' and 'no, sirs' would disappear and poor Eddie'd be heading for the door. And Pip here, she has a sense that we humans don't have. From day one she never liked this housekeeper that we thought was wonderful. Even Jake was convinced that if Mom liked her that much then she was okay. Three months later we caught her stealing leftover grocery money. And when we made a more thorough search, we found the bottom five checks gone from the checkbook. Pip had been right from the start."

"So, you don't think I could fool her, huh?"

"Not a chance."

"Good. Deception is way too complicated for me. I have a hard enough time not being overwhelmed by the truth. Distraction and avoidance are the best I can do when the truth is too much for me."

"It's unfortunate, though, some people would rather hear the lies, and it only makes the truth less palatable in the long run."

"So you're out at home and the university?"

Erin spoke as if to herself. "Why didn't I see that coming?" She chuckled softly and added, "I just realized how much I speak in generalities. No wonder Joyce gets so frustrated with me." She called to Pip to make the turn for home. "Joyce is Terri Sandler's partner. She nails me to the point all the time. The two of you would be something to deal with in the same conversation."

"You'd rather leave us to our assumptions? I did assume correctly that my realtor and my professor were sisters. That's made things so much easier for me. I want to find a way to thank you both."

"Not necessary. I've already had a fabulous Fratellini dinner out of this, and Terri will get her commission. Which reminds me . . ." They stopped on the little walk in front of the house, Pippin racing to the front door and back again when she realized that they had not followed her. Dhari bent down to fuss again and asked, "Will she let me pick her up?"

"She'll probably let you take her home."

Dhari picked her up, accepted little kisses over her lips and nose and returned kisses to the top of Pip's head. "Yes, I like you, too. You're just perfect," she said as the bat ears perked forward, "small and strong and sweet as can be." Dhari looked at Erin with a smile. "I've wanted a little dog as far back as I can remember. We could never have animals . . . because of Mom." She buried her face in the soft fur and hugged her before putting Pip down. "I'm sorry, Erin, I interrupted you. What were you going to say?"

"Oh, that I gave my recommendations to Terri over dinner. She'll fill you in when you meet with her."

"I won't be seeing her until Monday. Is there anything I could be doing over the weekend to expedite things? I'm not as pressed for time this trip since my boss is letting me work from here, but I may as well be getting something accomplished."

Erin opened the front door to let Pip in, then returned to

Dhari. "Depends on some decisions you'll be making. It wouldn't hurt, though, to set aside any official looking papers you come across, and old pictures of the house, especially dated ones."

"Yes, I meant to tell you that you were right about going through some of that stuff. I took a box home and I did find some documents. I want to show them to you. I need to know if papers like that should stay with the house."

Erin hesitated. She watched the neighbors pull into the drive across the street before turning back to Dhari. "All right. I'm not going to offer anything unless you specifically ask, though. I will stay out of your business. So, if you want an opinion you'll have to ask."

"Fair enough." Dhari retrieved her keys from her jacket pocket. "Will you come out tomorrow afternoon and let me fix you and Nessie lunch?"

"I think my schedule can handle that."

"Will you bring Pip?"

Erin raised an eyebrow. "The real reason I'm invited?"

Dhari merely smiled and turned on her heel. She's flirting. Among other things, that's what she's been doing, flirting. No kidding.

Chapter 17

The moon was only a sliver of a fingernail, the countryside blacker than anything Dhari had ever experienced. She gave up on trying to find her way around to the back door and stumbled up the front steps. After fumbling with the key and the door and deciding that her eyes could never adjust that much, she realized that leaving the headlights on until she got in the door and put the house lights on would have been the smart thing to do.

"This is why people live in civilization," she mumbled, feeling the wall for the old push button light switch. Good Lord, Nessie, how on earth do you make it home with no flashlight? "Finally," she exclaimed, pushing the button that lit the sconce lights in the hallway.

She peeked into the parlor as she passed; it was much as she remembered it from her last visit. The burl wood desk with its rolltop and display shelves, their treasures dustless behind glass doors, would be the first thing she'd clean out tomorrow. Any other official papers would likely be in there, and surely she could talk Nessie into taking what was in the display.

The switch to the living room was easier to find and bathed the room in a soft yellow glow. The room was warm and inviting and Dhari was beyond tired. Jetlag, she decided, was for real. All she wanted to do was sit completely still for a while. Besides, she should leave the lights on for a little while so that Nessie wouldn't worry that she was sick again.

Dhari wheeled her travel bag up next to the small round reading table, and pulled the platform rocker from the window to face the room. It was no Lazyboy, but it was much more comfortable than she had imagined. She sighed heavily and rested her head back. This has to be the quietest place on earth, she thought as she closed her eyes. I never thought anything could be this quiet. No highway hum, no squealing tires. Not a voice, or a cry, or a laugh, not even from the distance.

Something startled Dhari awake. She sat up, eyes wide open, confused and disoriented. She stayed perfectly still until she realized where she was, then listened carefully for what had awakened her. But it was disturbingly quiet. Dhari looked at her watch, two-thirty. She should be snuggled into the feather bed upstairs and deep in REM sleep.

Sorry, Nessie, I hope you're not waiting up for the lights to go off. Dhari forced herself out of the rocker. Dragging her bag behind her she shut off the lights as she left the room and trudged slowly up the stairs. They squeaked and groaned beneath tired, heavy feet. Although her intention all the way down the hall was to crawl into bed, clothes and all, she instead found herself standing before the old pedestal sink performing her nightly routine. Washing, brushing, grooming—it never varied no matter how tired she was. But it's necessary, it's just good hygiene, she told herself. Habit doesn't equal compulsion. Compulsion takes away choice and replaces it with useless tasks and wasted time.

This, however, is not useless. Nothing here is wasted time. She brushed her hair with deliberation, stroke after stroke, until it felt right to stop. She refused to count strokes. Never mind that a health magazine recommended a hundred strokes for shiny, healthy hair; exactly what Grandma Em had said years ago. Counting came way too close to what most people recognize as typical compulsive behavior. A behavior she would have to keep to herself, and not worth the worry. As long as it was within her control, people were going to see only what she wanted them to see.

What had happened tonight, another damn gumball drop from head to mouth, would not happen again. She'd been first-time lucky that Erin Hughes thinks the bones in her own closet shine just as bright white as hers. Most people, however, aren't that honest. They lock their skeletons up behind propriety and self-protection and make choices that to the casual observer seem entirely normal. Just like Dhari Weston. It's the closer inspection, the one that rattles the door, that has to be avoided.

Dhari returned her toiletries to their respective places on the back of the toilet, stuffed her dirty clothes into a laundry bag, and made one last glimpse into the mirror. What they see is all they get, she reaffirmed.

She'd spent years in thought over how to present herself to the world. Beyond tweaking the process now and then, there didn't seem to be much benefit in wasting additional time on it. But unlike most nights, tonight the time between consciousness and sleep, when her own heartbeat was the only sound and she felt most vulnerable, was filled with thoughts of Erin Hughes. Merely wondering whether she indeed formed more than an academic interest for the doctor was enough to stave off the usual fears that precluded sleep. Tonight, the little girl who is as afraid of herself as she is of being alone, fell asleep under the vision of Erin Hughes's smile.

In early morning darkness Dhari was once again startled awake. Again she listened, wide-eyed and intent. It was a creaking sound, similar to the creak of the stairs only higher in pitch. A door? She heard it again, and then seconds later again. Could it be a floor squeak? Barely moving her head Dhari looked around at unfamiliar shadows. She watched for movement. Nothing. She listened for the sound to get closer, or to fade. It did neither. She held her breath, tried to hear the direction of the sound over the pounding of her own heartbeat.

Someone breaking into a deserted house? No, the car is out front. She crept from the bed, moved as lightly as possible across the floor. Damned old creaky floorboards. She stopped to listen and heard the sound again. Nessie, maybe it's only Nessie. Oh, if only I could believe that. But she couldn't, not even enough to call out her name. Dhari chanced the creaking boards and started down the hallway close to the wall where there was less give to the floor. She passed the bathroom and peeked in carefully. The shadows had softened into a soft gray stillness; the day was beginning to dawn.

She stepped to the old spindle railing that surrounded the stairwell, leaned over it and listened. She remained there, motionless, for what seemed like minutes. This time the nearness of the sound startled her. It wasn't coming from downstairs, but rather from a room near the front of the stairs. A room she had not been in. Could it still be Nessie, moving about a room she was familiar with? Sorting through things? But so early. Why would anyone rise before dawn except to go to work?

And if it wasn't Nessie or an intruder? Well, they were the only explanations she'd allow herself to contemplate. There are no such things as ghosts. No such things.

Dhari stood before the closed door. Wouldn't it be wiser to sneak downstairs first and see if it looked as if someone could have gotten in? And safer? An open window, an unlatched door, and I'm out of here—in the car, down the road. She was about to turn, to take her own advice, when she heard the sound and with a rush of fear tainted adrenalin she burst into the room. Dhari looked quickly from one end of the room to the other, then focused on the source of the sound.

There, pressing against the windowpane, was a knurled finger from a branch of the old beech tree. Newly opened leaves caught enough of the wind to move it across the glass. Dhari released a long, slow breath. "Thank you," she whispered into the empty room. "Thank you."

"And you, are a goner," she added, straining unsuccessfully to lift the lower section of the window, "as soon as I get this damn thing open."

But the swollen wood of the sash held solid and Dhari gave up short of bruising her hands. As resolve set in, Dhari's focus changed, lingering on the old tree and beyond to the first flush of dawn. She stood in awe as the pale pink promise of a perfect day ripened to shades of peach and then deepened into an orange glow that rose from behind the field and bathed the old beech tree in brilliance.

It was a breathtaking sight, more beautiful than she had ever experienced. She moved from window to window along the east side of the house, upstairs and down, watching the sun silently announce the day, and totally forgot the fright that had awakened her. When she was satisfied that she had visited every angle and absorbed every minute, Dhari poured herself a glass of orange juice and took it to the sitting room.

She doubled the napkin to use as a coaster and placed the glass on the round reading table. True to last night's promise she would begin the day by sorting through the desk. As she reached for the arm of the rocker to pull it toward the desk, Dhari stopped in puzzlement. The rocker was facing the window. Hadn't she moved it from that very spot last night? Was it last night? Why can't I be sure? But if I were sure . . . She couldn't stop the feeling; it was old and too familiar—an unsettling confusion and fear. The same sickening feeling that drove her from her first apartment. She'd tolerated it for two months, two months of suspicion and self-doubt, worrying that the displaced items and strange smells were signs that she was crossing the line. Was she losing control, were they the manifestations of a distorted psyche? Fearing the worst, she had called on the pact and Douglas. It was his idea, matches tucked where they couldn't be seen, held tightly by each closed door and drawer, that proved it wasn't a wayward psyche but rather a perverted landlord that was responsible. He'd been making regular visits to her bedroom, her dresser drawers, her privacy. The craziness had been his.

And this, she decided with a deep breath, was just Nessie. Nessie with a key and a habit of coming in any time she felt like it. That's all.

She had given up trying to sort from the chair. Dhari sat on the floor in front of a now empty desk with piles of its contents all around her. The three small boxes she'd picked up at the grocery store were already full. Why did I think this would be easy? Her vow to skim and not read broke down soon after unused stationary and supplies had been boxed. She must have kept every card anyone ever sent her. And letters—no one writes like this anymore. You just pick up the phone.

"Oh, shit!" Dhari scrambled to her feet. "Jamie!" She ran up the stairs, grabbed the phone from her bag and dialed Jamie's number. "Damn," she said after the fourth ring, "please answer."

"Hello."

"I'm sorry, honey, I really am. I meant to call last night, but I got in so late and just fell asleep."

"A good time then?"

"I met Erin Hughes, the woman who's helping my realtor, for dinner and then she showed me around the town."

"Is there something you're not telling me?"

"Yes, there is," Dhari replied. Then after a pause she added, "I miss you. I wish you had taken a couple of vacation days and come down with me."

"Find a fun place to go and maybe I'll come down later in the week. My nephew's birthday is tomorrow; he'll be eight. Can't miss that," she said, then added with a chuckle, "Or the chance to send my sister into therapy."

"Just behave, Jamie. Don't give your sister reasons to

believe that your father is right. Besides, eight years old, he's old enough to realize that something's going on beneath the surface."

"I'll be careful. He loves his Aunt Jame; I won't do anything to jeopardize that. But, I'm not going to let his parents jeopardize it, either."

The sound of an engine and crunching gravel took Dhari to the front bedroom window. The Ram was nearing the top of the drive. Dhari checked the time. Erin was early.

"Well, don't concentrate so hard on pushing your sister's buttons that you can't enjoy your nephew," she said, halfway down the stairs.

"That's just it—enjoying him is pushing her buttons. I can't miss," she said, adding another chuckle.

Dhari opened the door and motioned Erin in the front. Pip was a silent blur, racing toward the side of the house after a squirrel as big as she. "Uh, huh," she said, with a smile directed at Erin.

"A visit long enough to eat a piece of cake, give him a present and pat on the head," Jamie was saying, "and leave before Dan gets home, is PC and barely within her tolerance."

"She has to know that's not going to happen." Dhari pointed toward the living room and followed Erin in. She touched Erin's arm and nodded toward her morning's efforts displayed on the floor.

"...on my way to find the computer games he wants," Jamie continued, "so that he can spend hours teaching me to play them. And eventually letting little brother play, not having cake and ice cream until after dinner, and watching Dan play his 'glad you came over' game very badly."

"Something I'm sure you'll enjoy way too much," Dhari replied.

Jamie was laughing on the other end; Erin was revisiting the pictures on the wall. "Will you call me tomorrow night?" Dhari asked.

"Sure you're not going to be too busy?"

The inference seemed out of character. Jamie the

confident, the sought-after, with no reason to doubt that she could hang on to someone like Dhari. The question was as irritating as it was felicitating. Dhari turned away and stepped toward the doorway. "I miss you," she said quietly, "and I'll be waiting for you to call . . . Okay. Have fun tomorrow."

"Well," Erin declared as Dhari returned, "I'd say it's a good sign when I see you smiling despite a morning of family bonding."

Dhari raised her eyebrows. "Not having to worry about my job is helping, and you certainly have made things easier." She held up the phone before placing it on the table. "And Jamie. My brother thinks I date her so that I don't have to pay for therapy."

Erin turned a fading grin toward the pictures again and spoke in a rather disconnected tone. "A doctor?"

"Oh . . . no. Jamie has her own insurance agency." Dhari walked closer to see what was so interesting to Erin. "But she has this way of dealing with her life, and a very messed up family situation, that is nothing short of incredible. I wish I were as strong, but I'm not. So, I ride along vicariously and let her make me laugh . . . hey, come here, I want to show you something."

Dhari retrieved a large envelope from the floor and handed it to Erin. She watched her pull from it a handful of articles neatly cut from newspapers. "You were right, Anna Grayson sure knew who I was. These are articles from my local papers—sports, spelling bees, school plays, musical events—anytime one of our names was in the news. She knew our interests, when my father joined the staff at the community college, when I took the position at Great Lakes, everything. And these," she picked up a smaller envelope and produced small, neatly trimmed articles announcing each of the children's births. "She even knew how much I weighed at birth."

Erin was sifting through the articles, briefly stopping here and there. "So, somebody must have been sending these to her."

"No," Dhari said as she pointed to a newspaper sitting on the table. "It really isn't any more complicated than this. It was in the box at the beginning of the drive, and there is a stack of them in the back room by the door."

Erin picked up the paper and smiled. "She subscribed to the papers wherever your family lived. I guess it's safe to say that it wasn't her lack of interest that kept you from knowing her."

Dhari scanned the piles of papers and the boxes and envelopes still untouched. "I wonder what other surprises are here somewhere?"

A sudden burst of insistent, high-pitched barking sent them both to the window, then out the door and into the side yard. There they found Pip as far along one of the beech's lowest branches as she could go, yelling back at a chattering squirrel sitting just out of her reach.

"Lord, Pippin," Erin exclaimed, "what would happen if you ever caught one?"

Dhari laughed as she watched a frustrated Pip dance precariously on tiptoes trying to find a way up a vertical part of the branch. The squirrel turned and began flicking its tail just inches from Pip's nose. Pip stretched and quivered and barked and finally turned to Erin for help.

"I know," Erin told her, "why would God give you the desire to chase something you can't catch? It doesn't seem fair, does it?" She reached above her head toward a reluctant Pip. "Come on, little girl, enough frustration for one day." Erin plucked the little dog from the branch and kissed her head. "There is not another tree that would have allowed you to get that close."

She delivered the tiny hunter to Dhari's outstretched hands where Pip immediately began telling her how happy she was to see her. Guttural sounds somewhere between growls and whines interspersed with fervent licks of her lips and nose made Dhari laugh. "Oh!" she exclaimed, tipping her head back. "I just got frenched."

"Yep, that may well be the quickest tongue in Atlanta."

"Only our second date, too," she said, nuzzling a kiss to Pip's neck before putting her on the ground. "Hey," she directed at Erin, "before I forget, do you see that branch up there, against the window?"

Erin ducked under the low limb to get a better look.

"I can't even describe to you the sound that makes when the wind moves it. Almost scared me Baptist this morning. Will you help me open that window after lunch so that I can break it back?"

Erin smiled at her. "Anything to save you from that kind of conversion. When will Nessie be here?"

"Soon," she replied, starting for the house.

"Are you a good cook?" Erin asked.

"Now you're asking to be scared," Dhari returned. "I'm closer to survivor than I am gourmet, but I do make a darn good fruit and nut tuna salad."

"It'll take more than that to scare me." Erin followed Dhari up the stairs. "My zucchini bread will be perfect then."

Chapter 18

While Nessie watched and Pip explored the upstairs, the old wooden sash was forced open and the wayward branch broken back.

"Things like this ever sit you up straight in the middle of the night, Nessie?" Dhari asked.

"Some, not long enough ago to forget." Nessie pursed her lips and wrinkled her brow into a frown. "When we was too young we prayed 'neath da blanket dat it wasn't ghosts we was hearing. When we was grown we prayed dat da noises in da night would only be ghosts."

"I can't pretend to know what that must have felt like, Nessie. I've known very little fear in my life," admitted Erin.

It was apparent to Dhari that there was more behind Erin's understanding than her own. In an effort to catch up, she asked, "What was it like, Nessie?"

Nessie shook her head. "Can't be told." Although it was still there, seared like a brand on the lining of her soul, the kind of fear that had haunted her through the many years could not be told to anyone. It was the kind of fear that could not be understood, only felt. And not even those who felt it could understand it. How is it possible to understand that the soul that your momma swore was God's eternal gift was worth no more than a day's worth of work by weary hands? That hopes and plans for a better future must be traded for justifying each day's survival, and that God's promise of eternal life was the only life that could be counted on? And that there was no protection—not the tolerant, loving relationship with a white family, not even owning your own land—against midnight dates with hatred?

"Well, speaking of ghosts," Erin said, breaking the silence. "Is this where Grandma Addy locked Billy up?" She indicated a large mahogany armoire, the finial of which nearly touched the ceiling.

Nessie nodded, and Dhari was sure that this time she wouldn't mind being left out of the conversation. Child abuse had not been her first suspicion about this part of the family, but it is on her list of don't-need-to-knows. She looked around the room for something else to concentrate on.

But Erin didn't allow it. "Do you mind if we open it, Dhari?"

"Oh, no. You and Nessie look through anything you want. I think I'll go downstairs and decide my next plan of attack."

"Don't you want to see if the Billy doll is still here?"

Of course, a doll. For once I kept my mouth shut at the right time. "Sure," she replied. "Is he a special doll?"

"Nessie says he was the reason for one of the ghost stories getting started about this house." Erin turned the key that was still in the keyhole and opened the doors. "I thought it would be good to dispel as many rumors as I could before you heard them."

"Yeah," Dhari replied, looking at a fairly normal collection of blouses and dresses and shoes, "there's a good idea."

"I don't see it, Nessie," Erin said. "Was it there on the top shelf?"

"Right dare," she replied, "high outta reach."

Erin pulled a footstool from beside the bed to the front of the armoire and stepped up to search the shelf. "No Billy," she reported.

"Too long ago. Miss Anna musta cleaned it out. Might be in da attic room."

"The attic was going to be my next plan of attack." Erin directed a wink a Dhari. "I can spend hours in an attic looking through people's oldest treasures."

"I'll show you where it is, den I'm going' home. Carletta's coming to take me shoppin'."

"If we find things we want to ask you about, we'll set them aside," Erin said following Nessie to the other end of the hall.

Nessie nodded and opened the door to narrow stairs that went up to the left and down to the right. "Servant's stairs," she said. "Goes up to da quarters and down to the kitchen." She grasped Dhari's arm as she turned to leave. "Tank you for da nice lunch," she said, looking up into Dhari's face.

"Thank you for being so helpful." Dhari followed an incredibly strong impulse and leaned down and hugged Nessie. "There's not enough thanks for taking care of me when I was sick."

Nessie kissed Dhari's check. "No need," she said, then turned and headed down the hall.

The impulsiveness of the hug surprised Dhari; there was very little hugging done in the Weston family. She could count hugs on one hand and have digits left for pinching. They'd never been a physically close family. But the tears surprised her even more, welling up in her eyes as she hugged the old woman. Dhari wiped them quickly before turning to face Erin.

"Is everything okay?" Erin asked, looking into still moist eyes.

"Yeah, fine. Let's go on up."

They climbed the stairs, found the switch to bare bulbs protruding from old porcelain fixtures and looked around. It was a full third story, wide open for the most part, with only partial walls partitioning one end. Furniture, and trunks, and boxes were stored everywhere.

"Where to," Erin stopped mid-sentence when she met Dhari's eyes. "What is it? What's wrong?"

"Nothing," Dhari said with an attempt at a smile. She tipped her head as though she was going to say something, but stopped.

"Something harder than telling me that your mother's crazy?"

Dhari sighed and shook her head. "I love that old woman."

Erin smiled. "Is that what a kiss to your cheek will do for a woman?" Since the remark was ignored, Erin added, "I love her, too."

"But I didn't want to. I didn't want to have her on my mind, to worry about her. She's so old, so far away."

Erin nodded. "And so special."

"I thought maybe she was a little crazy at first, asking me if I believe in ghosts. She still could be, I suppose. But it doesn't matter anymore."

"Do you really think believing in ghosts is crazy?" Erin asked. "What if Nessie was just testing to see if you were crazy?"

"That's not funny, Erin."

"I wanted to make you laugh. It was something that Jake probably could have gotten away with; but from me it came off as insensitive. I didn't mean it to."

Her tone was apologetic, her eyes sincere. The furrow between Erin's brows was the last bit of evidence that it took to convince Dhari that giving up her secrets so impulsively, at least the one slip to this woman, wasn't going to hurt her. No, Erin Hughes was not the kind of woman who would hurt anyone, not intentionally. And unintentionally, Dhari decided, could be forgiven.

Dhari looked around at what she knew was an insurmountable task, and chose to ignore it. "So, where do you think Billy is?"

"Hmm, if I were Anna Grayson clearing out a closet I wanted to use for myself, what would I do with the contents? Clothes and hats and things I wouldn't use I would probably give away. Whatever else was there—"

"But you have to know that she kept every card and letter that she ever got," Dhari added.

"Then I would have kept things with childhood memories. But would I pack them away in boxes or in trunks?"

"Let's try the trunks first," Dhari suggested. "They look easier."

They began with the closest and moved from one to the next, uncovering neatly folded linens and handmade quilts and too many crocheted pieces to count.

"How big do you think Billy is?" Dhari asked.

"I'd guess that Anna learned to make dolls from her mother or her grandmother, so I'd say that we're looking for one similar to the one that Nessie showed us."

Dhari stood and stretched her back. "And why is it important for you to find it?"

"I'm beginning to wonder that myself. I know Nessie wouldn't lie about it, and her memory seems sharper than mine at times." Erin searched the shadows and spotted the edge of a fourth trunk barely visible behind a large pie safe. "I guess I have to see it for myself. Here, help me move this, there's another trunk back here."

Together they maneuvered the cupboard with its contents of heavy crocks and bowls out into the room enough to reach the trunk. The leather handle, dry with age, gave way in Dhari's hand as they pulled the old round-top trunk clear.

"This has been here for a long time. I doubt if my aunt could have gotten to it."

Erin lifted the top. "I don't expect to find Billy in here."

Dhari held up the top, not trusting the hinge-stops to hold on their own, while Erin lifted out the tray. The lid and the tray were sectioned into a number of covered compartments and the whole interior of the trunk was lined with pristine flowered paper. Erin carefully opened each compartment and reverently examined its contents. There were handmade sachets and little jewelry boxes and a long white christening dress and its matching bonnet hand-fashioned of soft cotton.

"It does make me feel strange, looking through other people's things; like I want them to somehow tell me that it's all right to do it. I want them to hand me the things they kept and tell me what they meant to them." Erin handed Dhari a piece of fabric the size of a handkerchief. An undefinable woven design had been begun with shiny dark threads. "Like what is this? What made it special enough to keep; what memory did it hold?"

Dhari had no answer, but she was beginning to understand why Erin had to ask the questions.

She watched Erin lift a vintage wedding dress, fine lace and embroidery, from the bottom of the trunk. She laid it over her knee and ran her hand gently over the bodice. She was silent, deep in her own thoughts. Dhari clipped short her desire to ask and let Erin refold the dress and place it to one side uninterrupted.

Erin continued examining linens and clothing, replacing them neatly as if they should remain there indefinitely, until finally lifting her head to look into Dhari's eyes. "I've never had permission to look into my own parent's lives; my real parents. I wonder if they were married? I wonder if they ever think about me? What things were important to them? What would they have saved?"

Erin didn't move from her position on one knee, but she looked back down just in time to miss seeing the tears forming in Dhari's eyes.

Emotions tumbled and twisted, trying to identify them-selves as Dhari quickly wiped the tears clear. What is all this? she questioned. First Nessie, now Erin? I can't cry for my own family, but I can cry for these women? There is something terribly wrong here. She took a deep breath and regained control.

"Thank you," Erin said looking up briefly, "for letting me explore your family."

Dhari's smile blocked the way for any further tears. She knelt down beside Erin. "Let's see what's in the top." She chose a small compartment with a leather pull that contained a box of buttons and sewing and embroidery materials, while

Erin chose a larger one.

"Oh," Erin whispered, "look at this." She opened a leather pouch and withdrew a bundle of letters. She untied the leather thong holding them together, and read the addresses of the first few envelopes. "Find something to sit on," she said. "We just found Billy."

Chapter 19

Springhill, Georgia
25th of January 1864

My Darling Billy,

I send my highest hope that this finds you and your mother safe and well. I must admit that my understanding for your move to Pennsylvania is now complicated with my severe sense of loss. If not for the insane necessity of this war you would still be here, with your family unbroken and near to me.

This war is cruel and wrong but for the hope that at its end no human shall ever again be enslaved by another. My husband is wrong; yet, I do not judge him because he fights for the Confederacy that he believes in, but because what he believes in is an abomination. He fights to continue enslaving others as he enslaves his wife. I feel the stripes of slavery upon my back, even after the pain is gone. I see the fruits of my labor expected but not appreciated by my master. I hear my name spoken not in the tone of love or respect, but with that of condescension.

There are times when I fear that my spirit will bow for the last time and never again raise its head, and I know that I *should not allow myself to live to that point where hope is gone. But then I look into the eyes of dear baby Mary and I know that I must find a way to endure. If only it were possible for me to live my life with you.*

I plead you not join in this war in any way, but make a new life for your blessed mother and pray for a quick and merciful end to this war.

I remain your loving Adeline

Dhari, perched on the edge of a cardboard box, huddled close to Erin as they read the old letters. The script was at times difficult to decipher, due more to the penmanship than the dimness of the light, but they continued undaunted.

Pittsburgh, Pennsylvania
February the 19th, 1864

My Dearest Adeline,

Your safety is of my first concern. Although it was also of concern when your husband was at home, the circumstances of war are neither predictable nor controllable. The battles so near you now are rumored to be serious and this war shows no indication of ending soon. You and Mary are before all other thoughts. That harm could come to either of you is a possibility I cannot bear.

At present the 111th regiment is on veteran furlough, but are rendezvousing here in Pittsburgh and will travel by rail to Alabama. Cobham's troops fought well at Lookout Mountain and Ringgold, but have suffered many injuries and losses. They will welcome a new recruit, and I will welcome the chance to make my way to you.

Mother is enjoying good health and is well settled here. She has found good company at Mary Denby's boarding house, but her spirit is greatly saddened by the separation of our family. If not for the loss of her husband I dare say that she would not be here with me, as the whole of her family would weight the scale heavier than her private convictions.

I pray this will be delivered in quicker fashion than your letter came to me, as it took three weeks to arrive. Do not write me again until I write you and tell you where we are camped.

Your love is the thought that wakes me in the mornings and gives me cause to dream at night. I hold you in my heart until I can hold you in my arms.

Affectionately yours,
Billy T.

The look on Dhari's face made Erin smile. "A little like visualizing your parents having sex, isn't it?"

"She looks so prim and proper in the pictures."

"Calling her 'Grandma Addy' makes it even harder to imagine her in an affair," Erin added. "But that's not going to stop me from reading the rest of these letters; how about you?"

"I'm not quitting until I find out whose baby Mary is." Dhari reached for the next letter, not waiting for Erin, and opened it quickly.

Bridgeport, Alabama
March the 21st, 1864

My Dearest Adeline,

I am glad to finally have free time in which to write to you. We left Pennsylvania on February the 26th and the trip here would have been most unbearable if not for the thought that it was bringing me to you. We traveled in freight cars and the nights were so cold we had to build fires on the floor of the car to keep off the frostbite. We had to leave the doors partly open due to the smoke. Sleep was near impossible.

We arrived in Bridgeport on March the 9th and were pleased to find the weather warm and pleasant. But of late the nights have turned very cold and last night it began a steady snow that felled a plump foot by noon today, more than is noted in this area. But a full day's sun will do much to thaw us and brighten our spirits. Camp is set up now and is in good operation. We will be guarding this railroad, as it is the bloodline for men and supplies. It is quiet, easy work and our garrison is strong enough to defend against any attack. Do not worry for my welfare, as we are not likely to see any fighting at this present stage of war. It is still too far a distance to leave out alone, so I will wait and serve this army until it moves further south.

Please do write to me and direct your letters to Billy T. Phillips Co D 111th regiment PVV 2nd Division 20th A C Army of the Cumberland. I must write to Mother now so that she knows I am well and safe.

I am Affectionately Yours,
Billy T.

Springhill, Georgia
3rd of April 1864

My Darling Billy,

You have put my heart in such a state of agitation. It swells blissfully at the thought of your love, yet it shrinks in terror at the danger you face. How could I live without the hope of a life someday with you? You have revived it in my life; for once married to my husband I had lost the hope I once had.

I give my tears for you free rein now that the captain has his command in McPherson's army. I am free of the fear of hiding them for as long as he is gone. If only I could have fled with you, to be free of this bondage. But it could not be, and it is a stone upon my heart that I know it. This land is my *responsibility and I cannot shun it. Likewise, the Negroes here have given their hearts and souls to it and without me it could be gone from them as well. That shall be my peace if there is to be any at all for me.*

Since Father's death at Chattanooga last year I have tried to convince Mother to move here to the big house with me. She has finally agreed to abandon the small house to one of the Negro families; it is much needed by them. Mother knows the workings of the farm as well as Father and is of great assistance. With the loss of the men we have become stronger for each other.

I have heard nothing recent of your brothers' welfare. I know that General Johnston's army has been continuously engaged by Sherman, but word of the wounded is slow in coming, and it may be good news that I have heard nothing. This is a wretched war for which I set blame on the inability of men to entertain change for the overall good of this world. I cannot wish injury or death to either side, only a swift and sure end to the bloodshed.

I send you my love, for it is all I can do. Little Mary and I are safe, and I am going about the duties required of me here.

Your loving Adeline

"Are you familiar with the battles and the generals they mentioned?" Dhari asked.

Erin nodded as she opened the next letter. "More familiar than I am with the faculty I work with." She looked up as she realized Dhari's confusion, then patiently explained who was who and how the outcome of the battles affected the war.

"So Billy fought for the Union while his brothers fought for the Confederacy."

"This was a war that not only split families in their convictions, but physically impacted them permanently. Because we were fighting ourselves, the Civil War claimed nearly as many American causalities as all other American wars combined.

The losses were astronomical. But, the good thing," Erin added, "was that we ended it, once and for all, and unlike so many other countries, have never gone to that measure again."

"Civil strife, but not war."

"We've been able to tolerate the conflict necessary for social reform without it escalating into war. A remarkable achievement, really."

Remarkable, Dhari thought, a pretty good description of Dr. Hughes, too, I could add. So well studied—all that knowledge about things I know nothing about. What made her so determined, so passionate? She was studying Erin's face, focused, a childlike astonishment emanating from her face. Erin read unaware until Dhari realized that she had some catch-up reading to do before Erin changed pages.

Bridgeport, Alabama
April the 25th, 1864

My Dearest Adeline,

You must know that I relieve my own agitation with the thought that you are a smart woman and strong, and that you and your household are still safe and well. But that thought never stays long enough to rest itself permanent, and I am reminded that it is not only my desire to be with you that keeps me on my course. I must see with my eyes that you are safe and lend my strength to you to ensure it.

My health is good and the only disagreeable weather is some rain today. Spring is evident in the woods turning green. We have plenty of rations of the best quality with a bakery right here at the post, and if it were not for my desire to continue on to you, there would be nothing that would suit me better than to hold this position.

General Geary, who is in charge of this post, keeps us as busy as possible building and strengthening forts. There are seven to date and orders from General Thomas to build *another. I cannot imagine any position being any stronger or any greybacks catching us unaware. General Slocum moved out of here on the 11th to take command of Vicksburg. General Hooker has taken command of the consolidated 11th and 12th corps and they are now the 20th Army Corps and he has them scattered all along the railroad from Nashville to Chattanooga.*

There are rumors of the 111th moving further south soon, but nothing sure yet. If we do move or see any hard fighting this summer it will be up to General Sherman. Right now the troops being sent to the front are the colored regiments.

I will write you again soon. With all the shifting of commands and movement I should know something sure before long. Have still heard nothing of Jack or James.

Affectionately,
Billy T.

The two women remained huddled together in the dim light late into the night, reading letter after letter, with Pip curled and asleep in Erin's lap. The letters, dated from May 14th to June 24th, documented the movement of Billy T. and the 111th from Bridgeport to Tilton Station, to Pine Chappel south of Dalton, to Kingston, and on to the camp in the field near Big Shanty, and finally to Marietta. The fighting on the Western front had escalated and the 111th was actively engaged in continuous fighting under General Hooker. The 65,000 ill-fed and ill-equipped Confederate forces under the command of General Johnston attempted to stay between Sherman and the railroad behind them. They systematically gave up one entrenched position after another and success-fully avoided a full field battle that Sherman's 100,000 troops would have won easily, and kept them from Atlanta. But when President Davis lost patience with Johnston's failure to take the offensive and replaced him with General Hood, the fate of the South was sealed.

They unfolded and read the last letter.

Camp in the woods
Near Chattahoochee River
July the 15th, 1864

My Dearest Adeline,

The past few days have been the longest rest we have had since the beginning of this campaign. I write this not knowing if it will arrive to you before I do. I suspect we are as close as I could hope for, since we can see the steeples of Atlanta from climbing near the tops of the trees on the hill. We are about seven miles out on the north side of the river.

The rebel position at the river looks to be a strong one, built on the backs of five to ten thousand Negroes, and I have no idea how long Sherman will rest us here before challenging it. We were 500 strong leaving Bridgeport, with barely 200 now left to fight. I do know that when I light out it will be in the dead of night and without shred of evidence of this army or the other. I will arrive to you with a canvas bag at my side as a journalist seeking rest. I cannot tell you when, but pray it will be soon.

Affectionately,
Billy T.

Dhari's head snapped up. "Well he made it, didn't he?"

"Must have," Erin replied. "It's the most logical explanation for all of these letters being together." She looked again at the date of the last letter. "And just in time it seems."

"Why?"

"Hood surprised Sherman's troops with an offensive at Peach Tree Creek on the 20th. Initially it was a slaughter—ten percent of the Union's soldiers were killed."

"God," Dhari exclaimed. "He must have been able to hear

the gunfire; he must have known what was happening."

Erin looked into Dhari's eyes, shining in the dimness like the bare bulbs hanging from the rafters. "We're a pair," she said with a smile. "Rooting for a deserter and a guy who was doin' Miss Addy behind her husband's back."

"We don't know that they ever did it." The look she received punched right through the paper-thin rationalization, so she owned up. "I guess that doesn't fly if I'm questioning who fathered the baby."

"As I was saying," Erin said with a wink, "we're both rooting for him and neither of us is going to be satisfied until we find out what happened." She placed Pip on the floor, then stood with a groan. "How long have..." She tilted her watch toward the light. "No wonder I'm creaking like these old boards; it's almost two o'clock."

"Oh, we've probably worried Jake."

"He's fine," Erin assured her. "I told him that I might be late; he's been asleep for hours. Pip, though," she lead the way to the stairs, "is probably trying to open the front door by herself."

They found Pip as expected dancing impatiently at the door. She barely made it down the front steps, claimed the first corner of grass, and relieved a very full bladder.

"I'm sorry little girl," Erin said. "You have a horrible mom today."

But forgiveness came as quickly as the empty bladder. Pip, excited that she had the attention of both women, began racing in circles, wider and wider, ears flat against her head, little legs at full stride. She was half barking and half grunting, and running as fast as she could until both Dhari and Erin were laughing and clapping their encouragement.

When she finally tired, Pip raced up the steps and stood on her hind legs, resting one front paw against the door. With her nub of a tail at full wiggle, she turned her head to see if her cheerleaders had followed.

"See," Erin said with a grin, "I told you she'd go home with you."

"It's a good thing I'm not living here, or you might not get her back. She's pure joy."

"For such a tiny thing she sure does command your attention. And when you give her your full attention, you forget that you have anything else to worry about. She was a great comfort for Mom. She'd get Mom laughing to the point of tears sometimes, and it was wonderful to hear her laugh like that." Erin fished the keys from her pocket and called for Pip.

"Hey," Dhari said, taking Erin's arm, "why don't you stay the rest of the night. There's no sense in going home now, you'll just wake Jake."

"Are you up for more attic duty tomorrow?"

Dhari started up the stairs as she spoke. "On the hunt for Billy," she said raising her fist in the air.

Erin followed her through the door, her decision obviously made. "With Nessie's help this time."

Chapter 20

Erin, dressed in one of Dhari's T-shirts, was settled comfortably in Grandma Addy's bed. Pip was snuggled in the crook of one arm while Erin reexamined the letters by the light of a bedside lamp.

The sound of Dhari's voice at the bedroom door sent Pip to the side of the bed with ears wide and nub wagging.

"Come in," Erin replied. "I'm still up."

"I saw that the light was on, and I had forgotten to get a bowl of water for Pip." Dhari placed the bowl on the floor beside the door.

"She's a little tentative about the steps down from the bed, but she'll let me know if she has to get up for anything."

Dhari motioned toward the letters. "I can't stop thinking about them, either. They're something, aren't they?"

"A treasure better than gold to my thinking. Not just dates and events in history, but firsthand reactions and descriptions," Erin moved to make room for Dhari, "and emotions. It makes it all so personal. God, we even know what it felt like on a particular day—snow, rain, spring in bloom—I'm still discovering what it means to be holding them in my hands and reading the words."

Dhari stepped up and sat on the edge of the bed. "They're yours."

"Oh, no way, Dhari."

"I want you to have them. The look on your face as you read them is all I need to keep. Like Nessie said," Dhari placed her hand over her heart, "I keeps special gifts right here."

Erin shook her head. "I can't accept that, I'm sorry."

"Then keep them for me. I wouldn't know what to do with them except store them somewhere, probably in a place I would soon forget." The look on Dhari's face indicated that she was pretty pleased with herself at outmaneuvering the professor.

"You are an exasperating woman, Dhari. Miss Scarlet on the back of a mule."

Dhari laughed. "Is that one of Jake's?"

"Right out of Jacob Hughes's *The South as I Say It*," she joked.

"He makes me smile."

"Me, too. He's a special guy. And when I think about how special, it makes me feel bad for wishing these letters were mine, telling me about my blood family—where they came from, what they thought and felt."

"You shouldn't feel bad about that. It's obviously important to you; I'm sure Jake understands that."

"I don't know that he does. My mother definitely did not. There's very little that I fear, really—a man behind the wheel of a car with a cell phone at his ear . . ."

Dhari chuckled.

"Little else," Erin continued. "But I fear hurting Jake. If I made a list of the most important qualities parents must have, he and my mother would exceed each one. To chance hurting him would be an act of unadulterated selfishness."

"But if he doesn't know how much you want to find them, how can he let you know that it wouldn't hurt him?"

"I've given him many opportunities to offer whatever he knows, but . . . it's possible that he just doesn't know anything."

"It's also possible that he's the one who's being selfish," countered Dhari. "I say that with no disrespect, because I can say it about my own mother. By refusing treatment she deprives her husband of uncompromised intimacy of a truly honest relationship, her real self; it deprived her children of the basic nurturing necessary for healthy growth. And, it now deprives her grandchildren of the wise and loving guidance that only a grandmother can give. Nevertheless, I still love my mother and no matter what probably always will. Accepting that your father is being selfish doesn't mean that you love him any less."

"He has his faults, I know," Erin said. "But I just can't accept that that's one of them."

Dhari leaned back against the extra pillows piled at the footboard. Pip, seeing her chance, wrapped herself around Dhari's arm, and began licking the back of her hand.

"It's a nightly ritual," Erin explained, "some kind of bonding thing, I think. If it bothers you—"

"No, she's fine." Dhari fluffed the downy hair on the little dog's head. Pip, lifting only her eyes, continued licking uninterrupted.

"If those were your letters—your family," Dhari began, "what would you do with what you found out—I mean, how would you process it?"

"Would I see it as scandalous, you mean?"

"Yeah," Dhari replied, her brow pressed into a serious line. "Would you wish you hadn't found it out?"

"Do you really think any family is free of skeletons? They've all got them if you open enough doors. Affairs are so common that they are almost to be expected. The damage comes when a child results and is not acknowledged, and the secret is kept above all. Uncovering the secret should be most important."

Dhari pushed a pillow under her neck and laid her head back. "I think there are things that are better kept secret," she said staring at the ceiling.

"Like what?"

Dhari thought for a moment. "Anything that would make someone feel less loved, less capable, anything that would limit their dreams for the future."

"Such as?"

"A father finding out that a child isn't his, which could cause him to treat that child differently than his own blood children. A child knowing that they tested low on an I.Q. test that might erroneously define him for all time. An affair that was a mistake and if known would wreak havoc on an otherwise good marriage . . . I could go on."

"I might agree with you on the I.Q. test," Erin admitted. "But for the most part, I think secrets do more harm than good. Think about the damage that guilt can do—worrying if and when your extramarital liaison would be found out, continually hating yourself and wanting to be forgiven. How do you think that would affect that otherwise good marriage? And think about the genetic and health reasons for knowing who your parents are. Those reasons alone should outweigh the emotional risk, don't you think?"

When there was no response, Erin sat up and looked to the end of the bed. Pip opened her eyes but did not stir from her position against Dhari's chest. And Dhari, eyes closed and lips slightly parted, was equally still.

"Well, Pippin," Erin whispered, "at least they stay awake in my lecture hall." She smiled at Dhari, sleeping peacefully. "Someday maybe the secrets won't be so scary."

The sun had debuted hours earlier without notice. Dhari sat on the edge of the bed staring at the woman lying next to her. The morning air was cool, causing a sudden shiver as it brushed over the warm, moist skin of Dhari's face and neck. She barely noticed. Her mind was completely engaged in the thoughts she so long ago encountered in adolescence, thoughts gangly and awkward, stumbling over each other in need of identification. Years ago, lying on the floor next to her best friend at a sleep over, the same forbidden thoughts had emerged.

All the others are asleep; no one would know. What would

she do if I touched her lips with mine? Would it startle her, surprise her to open her eyes and find mine? Or would her eyes remain closed while her lips, soft and warm, accept mine without question ... opening into mine, pressing and giving back with equal ardor? Dhari questioned whether she dared such a move now just as she had questioned it long ago.

Back then there had been no thought past a kiss, no knowledge of the pleasures beyond—of heat and wetness and the fires of desire. She knew nothing then of the need that defies all reason, or the power of a woman's touch, or of ecstasy that it creates. She knew only that she wanted to be as close to her best friend as she could be—forever. Unlike now, when she knew that a kiss to Erin's lips could easily be a prelude. That if the warmth and growing excitement she felt around Erin was mutual, a kiss would surely turn warmth to passion—a friend to a lover—wondering to knowing.

She wondered what kind of lover Erin Hughes would be—tender and patient, letting first-time tentativeness build to an unbearable tension? Or would she be tenacious, commanding, sparking an explosion as sudden and fierce as a firestorm? She had never similarly wondered about others. No one had quite piqued her interest in the same way. There had been no confirmations or disappointments because there had been no expectations. The experience was whatever it was and had lasted for as long as it lasted. But today, she wondered.

What if I drew my fingertips gently over Erin's face and carefully kissed her eyelids open? What would she see in my eyes? Would she see something there that would make her draw me into the warmth of her arms and the sweetness of her mouth? What would keep our bare thighs, smooth and flushed, from pressing together beneath the down cover, or keep our aching breasts from bursting with excitement until their tips were firm?

It was easy, too easy, to fantasize it. And then to go beyond, to let sensations of heat go coursing through her body, seeping and pooling, from thoughts of imagined responses—Erin welcoming the touch of Dhari's hands, whispering her desire, gasping her pleasure. She could go on—wanted to go on—to the breathlessness, the desperation . . . Stop, she commanded herself. I cannot, will not go there.

So why such thoughts now? Now when a kiss is not just a kiss, and old adolescent thoughts carry with them a very serious adult quandary. She had always thought that being in a real relationship meant that even thinking about sex with someone else was cheating. It was an easy thing to believe during those young idealistic years, and to expect the same of others. During a time when what presented themselves as relationships lasted only months and no one knew anymore than she what would last and what would not. A time before fears became so real and inherited insanity didn't have such long-term effects.

But then came adulthood, the possibilities and opportunities for long-term relationships, and eventually, Jamie Bridgewater. Cheating became a relative term, open to a much broader interpretation than she had expected, and her definition of a relationship had been redefined. Honesty took the place of fidelity and someone else's needs and happiness became a priority.

It all seemed to be working. She had found someone who liked being with her, who satisfied her sexually, and who, she was convinced, would never stay in an unhealthy relationship. What more could she ask for? A fantasy now and then? An indulgence here and there? Merely a thought at the moment, as she focused again on Erin's face. But if she allowed it to develop . . . it would be the first time she had tested her new definition for herself.

They had no commitment, she and Jamie, so would there be guilt, she wondered? Or, would it be an experience to be treasured? She studied Erin's face. It was a wonderful face, she realized, smooth and clear and finely featured. The brows were higher and more meticulously groomed than her own, the lashes darkened and slightly curled. But it wasn't the structure of it, as fine as it was, that had captured Dhari's interest from that first day in the lecture hall. It was far less tangible. It had something to do with the way her eyes came from some distant place, mysterious and yet solemn, to focus so intensely on Dhari's. She felt as though something Erin saw there was more interesting, more important to her than all the rest of the world. At other times the assumption of being the center of Erin's world, if even for the moment, seemed almost arrogant; yet, the feeling returned, unashamedly, the very next time Erin looked at her. It was that feeling, Dhari decided, that allowed otherwise presumptuous thoughts of intimacy to intrude on conscious thought. Your fault, Dr Hughes, Dhari thought, for making me feel like this—like something more special than I am.

Erin stirred slightly, but didn't wake, as Pip wiggled into the crook of her arm. Pip sighed and closed her eyes. Dhari smiled at the little creature, so safe, so thoroughly content. No worries past finding her favorite toy or convincing her human that going for a ride is essential. Do humans ever experience such trust, such tranquility, such freedom from guilt?

"How long have you been awake?" Erin's eyes were suddenly opened, looking into Dhari's.

"Oh," Dhari replied, "a few minutes. I hope I didn't wake you." Thank goodness thoughts can't be heard.

Erin straightened onto her back and stretched her arms over her head. "No. I think I was dreaming. But when I wake I rarely remember what I dreamt." She gently stroked Pip's belly who had also stretched onto her back. "So," she said at the end of a yawn. "What's the agenda for today?"

There was a loud growl from Dhari's stomach. "Brunch first," she said with her hand on her stomach. "And phone calls, we'd better both make some phone calls. Then, let's take the letters over to Nessie and see what she has to say."

Chapter 21

"How old do you think Nessie is?" Dhari asked over her shoulder.

Erin followed behind her along the footpath leading from the Grayson house across the field to Nessie's. "My best guess? Over ninety, shy of a hundred."

"I wonder how many trips it takes to keep a path this worn?"

"I'd bet that Nessie has made this trip daily for—I couldn't even guess how many years—probably since she was a child. Maybe that's why she's in the shape she's in and I'm breathing hard."

"This is one long hike. I'll be loading whatever I can talk Nessie into keeping into the car and driving it over."

"You had seriously contemplated anything else?" Erin asked with a grin.

"Ah . . . no, not really."

They emerged from the end of the path into a yard no larger than could be maintained by a great-grandchild on a Saturday morning. Its boundaries were straight edges abutting the tall grass and shrubs of the surrounding fields. Flowerbeds, simple rectangles with green tips of spring growth pushing through the mulch, wrapped the front and side of the little white house.

"This is so Nessie," Erin declared. "Keeping her part of the world clear and manageable."

An incisive assessment, Dhari thought, culled from so little data. Is that how you assess all people, Dr. Hughes, drawing equally accurate assessments from so little? How would Jake say it? Clear as crystal right through dirty windows. Dhari smiled to herself. And how do you see me, Dr. Hughes? As someone who is too busy looking inward to see who others are? No doubt you recognized that before I did.

They had followed Nessie through the house and settled at the kitchen table where Erin proceeded to cut up the last of the fresh fruit and introduced Nessie and Dhari to peanut butter apples.

"I never would have thought so, but this is really good." Dhari reached for another slice of apple, spread it with peanut butter and silently marveled at how Nessie managed to eat them so easily without top teeth.

"It's a Jake thing," Erin admitted.

Dhari licked her fingers. "I should've guessed as much."

"According to Jake, most food can be greatly enhanced with a little peanut butter. That includes pancakes, ice cream, sugar cookies, and sandwiches with lettuce and mayonnaise."

Nessie just nodded as she closed her lips around a very large strawberry, making Dhari think that this, too, could be a southern thing.

"Mm," Erin mumbled as she rose quickly. "Keep munching, I've got to wash these hands before I touch those letters."

"Nessie," Dhari asked, "did Anna know about the letters from Billy?"

"Don't know," Nessie replied. "But she knew da secret sure nuff."

Before Dhari could ask another question, Erin had returned to the table, repositioned her chair next to Nessie, and carefully unfolded the first letter. With her audience at full attention, she began.

She read with feeling and emphasis, she became the voice of Addy and her lover from so long ago. A story more alive now than when they had read it up in the attic. As she listened, Dhari watched Nessie's face. Nessie's eyes were riveted on Erin. She sat motionless, listening to every word, a piece of apple still held in her hand. She was a world away. Remembering, Dhari imagined, things she'd been told when she was just a girl. Putting the pieces together, filling in the empty spaces.

Dhari lowered her gaze, then closed her eyes for a moment. There in her mind was Adeline from the picture on the sitting room wall. The words were hers, the voice could be too, saying them aloud as she wrote them to the man she loved. Intonations of hope rang out, hope for a future she only dared to imagine, for a love that would bring her the happiness she longed for. She tried to picture Billy. Was he sandy-haired and clean-shaven? Was his hair dark, his eyes deep-set and serious? There was no way to know, but it didn't matter. His words told more about him than any picture could have. He had taken control of what he could—took his mother to safety, braved the dangers of war to get to the woman he loved. Real dangers, proven dangers—no abstract fear or unfounded worries. He knew what he was facing and he faced it willingly for her.

When it was that she had opened her eyes and refocused on Erin she couldn't say, but the letters had all been read and Erin was folding the last one into its envelope. Erin's face was flushed and she had fallen silent.

It was Nessie who broke the silence. "Da secret's gonna break your hearts," she said looking from one to the other.

Erin expressed both their surprise. "I thought Billy was the secret."

"Only part."

Dhari shook her head. "I don't want to know."

"Then you'd better leave," Erin said, "because I'm going to hear it."

Dhari's heart picked up a beat. She pushed back her chair and looked again at Nessie. The old woman's eyes urged her to stay. Nessie stretched her hand across the table, and something made Dhari take it. She resettled in her chair and said nothing.

Erin spoke before Dhari could change her mind. "What happened, Nessie?"

"Da story came up from my grandma and my momma, and da same from Anna's," she said. "Dey picked Anna and me to know."

"And you picked us?" Erin asked.

"It needs tellin'," Nessie said with a squeeze of Dhari's hand. "Can't take it to my grave."

Erin was impatient. "Billy made it to the house or we wouldn't have the letters. Was Adeline there, or was he met by soldiers?"

"She was dere. Saw Billy sure nuff. Don't know how much time dey had—not much. Da fightin' at Peach Creek was real bad, real close to here. Might a been what brought da Captain back, don't know."

"Shit," Dhari whispered.

Nessie nodded. "He saw 'em together, right dere by dat tree—shot Billy dead."

"Oh, no," cried Erin.

Dhari let go of Nessie's hand and slumped back in her chair. The vision was far more disturbing having read the letters.

"Da rifle was always close," Nessie continued. "Protection from marauders leanin' against da tree. S'pose da Captain never counted on dat. Never figured his wife'd have da grit, but she did. Picked up da gun and shot him."

Dhari couldn't keep the vision from her mind—Adeline dropping to her knees, pulling Billy to her. Maybe he was already dead, maybe he was dying. Hopeless now, all was lost. Dhari shook her head. "How did she go on?"

"Somethin' inside," Nessie replied, "bent over tight as a willow branch, but it never snapped."

"And nobody knew?" Erin asked.

"Her momma. And my great-grandaddy. Charles was dere head Negro; he did da buryin'. Adeline took da shovel herself

138

to help put Billy to rest under da tree."

"Under the witness tree?" Dhari asked.

Nessie nodded. "Nobody knows where Charles put da Captain. Don't s'pose dey would a much cared. Dey was jus' glad livin' was easier when da Captain didn't come back from da war."

"And Adeline deeded part of the land to Charles," Dhari added.

"But dere wasn't a need to," Nessie said. "Da Negroes knew how to keep a secret."

A secret, Dhari was convinced, that would have been better kept.

"Nessie was right." She spoke to Erin who was ahead of her on the path.

Erin stopped and turned. "About what?"

"It broke my heart."

"Yes," Erin replied in a saddened tone, "mine, too." She stepped beside Dhari and put her arm around her shoulders. "I sure wish Addy and Billy could have had a life together."

Dhari made no attempt to move from the comfort of Erin's embrace. She walked along next to her, hands in her pockets. "You see what I mean? I didn't need to know that. The letters were enough."

"I know it's sad, and it's more comfortable for us to go along imagining the best. But unless we know the heartache Addy suffered, we would never know the strength of her character."

They walked along silently for a few minutes until a hazy, half-thought cleared itself. "You have to risk disappointment to get the color of passion."

Erin frowned. "I'm not sure, but I think we may be saying the same thing."

"Well, my boss is anyway. We can't appreciate the highs in life if we've never felt the lows. Lessons he learned from a movie that he took too lightly at first. I guess I was listening better than I thought."

"Or," Erin added, "it's suddenly relevant... that's why I try to tie my lectures to something current, something relevant—so they'll remember."

"I didn't need to know why she deeded the land away, though. Wouldn't you have rather thought that it was a righteous act on her part instead of bribery?"

"Of course. But it was a complicated time. That Nessie's family was kept together, that they felt enough loyalty and responsibility to stay to that point was a testimony to Addy and her parents... I wonder if Addy hadn't killed the Captain if eventually the slaves would've done it."

"Hmm, somehow that thought makes me feel better."

"Me, too," Erin said with a smile. "But, I think I wouldn't mind playing with Pip for a while before we do any more attic work."

"That would be your only hope of getting me back up there," Dhari replied, "and it's a slim one."

Chapter 22

They did return to the attic, but only after Pip's walk and a fetch game with a little cloth Frisbee, and a promise to sort safe stuff like furniture and dishes. The personal things would wait until Tuesday when Erin promised to return again.

Today, Dhari had awakened to the realization that it was decision making time. She sat in Terri Sandler's office trying not to seem overwhelmed.

"I know that's a lot of information all at one time, but we're trying to work within your time frame." Terri handed her a folder of papers and explained, "This is everything we just talked about. There are copies of Erin Hughes's recommendations, plus I've included application forms for the National Register nomination and insurance."

"She's very thorough, isn't she?"

"I must admit that even I was a little overwhelmed at first. But, I don't think the decision is as complicated as it looks."

Dhari was looking at page after page, but not much was registering clearly in her mind. "I sure hope you are seeing something I'm not."

"I am. Here's my suggestion. First, let's make sure we don't have a battlefield in the acreage. I should have that answer tomorrow. Then, let's get a survey done, so that we can have the house and some surrounding acres clearly defined and separated from the rest."

"And put the land on the market first."

"Yes. That buys you time to make other decisions and eventually you'll make more money."

"That's what you would do if you were me?" Dhari asked.

"Well, I'm not you," Terri replied, "but if Terri Sandler had inherited that property, she'd be dividing it up into smaller parcels and selling it a little at a time." She cocked her head slightly. "I'd be using it as an investment, not a one-time windfall."

"Hm," Dhari flipped back through the pages on her lap. "Erin didn't even think of that."

Terri rumbled into a laugh. "That's why I get that nice commission."

Dhari grinned her embarrassment. "Of course I didn't mean that the way it sounded. I just meant—"

"I know what you meant. The doctor is very thorough."

Relief was instantaneous. "Actually," Dhari began, "I like the idea—the smaller parcels—and having more time to make decisions. I'm liking not being stressed."

"I can see that. You are considerably more relaxed than the last time you sat here."

"I've realized how terribly I hate change, disruption; it throws me into a panic. I worry about everything coming apart—one little movement starting a domino chain, and everything going out of control. I want you to know how much I appreciate being able to count on you."

"Everyone likes to know that they're appreciated. Now," Terri added, "we need to discuss some unpleasantries. The survey is going to be expensive, I'll get the best price I can for you, and you'll have to come up with some tax money soon. That makes it important to get one parcel on the market as soon as we can. Meantime—"

"I need to apply for a short-term loan," Dhari concluded.

"I'll get the figures together for you for tomorrow."

"So," Dhari said as she rose, "that's that. No valium needed, no emergency therapy . . . unless there's something you haven't told me."

"No, nothing." Terri eased her formidable size around the desk to walk Dhari out. "Oh," she remembered, "except we're having Erin over Wednesday night, dinner and good company, and we would like to have you join us."

"Oh, I'd love to. What should I bring?"

Terri smiled and put her hand over Dhari's shoulder and squeezed gently. "You've just scored one on the Fratellini scale."

Chapter 23

Dhari tried Jamie's number again. It was true what she had told Terri Sandler about enjoying less stress, but less didn't mean no stress. There was still the convincing of her siblings to visit their mother on her birthday; and it had to be done by phone because there wouldn't be time once she got home. And there was Jamie—not in her office on a Tuesday afternoon and now not answering her cell phone. The anxiety that that alone caused was making her restless. It was business, of course. Not all transactions take place in an office. Nothing to worry about. Can't expect a businesswoman to be at beck and call—shouldn't expect anyone to be for that matter. Dhari stopped the call without leaving a message. She checked the time—six o'clock was well into personal time. Yesterday was family time, but what keeps her from answering the phone today? How much of what she does is even my concern? What is the scope of an unspoken commitment, especially now?

She dialed Jamie's number again and paced the floor of the sitting room until the voice mail answered.

"Hey, it's me," she said trying not to sound too irritated. The tone says more than the words. "I tried you at the office a couple of times. Hope everything is okay. Give me a call as soon as you can." Keep it short—no guilt trips, nothing to make her hesitate to call right back. She had heard those messages all her life. The ones left for her father full of angst and desperation, spoken in an accusatory tone and meant to generate guilt. Where are you? I'm so worried. I don't know what to do about Dana, or Douglas, or dinner. It didn't matter— anything to get his attention. Call after call, growing louder and increasingly more frenetic until the dementia was obvious even to a nine-year-old Dhari. I know what you're doing! Why? Why are you doing this to me? You don't care if I die, if we all die. Is that what you have planned, for us all to die so you can be with your whore? Where are you? I hate you! I hate you!

But he would come home from work as if he hadn't heard them. And Lela would have calmed and fixed dinner and made his favorite dessert. And Dhari would wonder why.

Later, when she was older, she would wonder how he had kept the messages from being heard by others. Had he always had an office by himself? He wasn't always a department head, how was it that no one heard? Or did they hear, and merely decided to leave the poor man with the crazy wife alone? Yet, how many times might they have believed that the crazy messages were true and judged her father responsible? There were just too many questions that would probably never be answered. She hated thinking about them. Douglas was at least partially right—I am with Jamie because she will never allow me to put her through that.

She had finally settled in to make some progress on work matters that she had hoped to finish before dinner when the phone rang.

Dhari jumped and picked it up after the first ring.

Jamie's voice was surrounded by background laughter. "Hey, Babe, everything okay?"

"This doesn't sound like a good time to talk."

"Just a minute," Jamie said before the phone was muffled. "I couldn't hear—okay, I'm back."

Dhari tried to keep her tone as light as possible. "What's going on?"

145

"We're helping a friend of Rosie's move, remember? The Keystone Cops meet Barbie." Jamie laughed. "Not a very efficient operation. I think she wishes that she'd hired Two Men and a Truck."

"Should I call you later?"

"No, there's no telling how long this'll take; we're having to help pack and move. Damn, I've never seen so much sally stuff in my life—I don't know how many boxes of dishes and jewelry and cosmetics and other frou-frous I packed. I didn't know they made that many colors of nail polish."

The thought of Jamie packing someone's frou-frous made Dhari smile. "Have I met her?"

"She was at the Christmas party—red dress, red lipstick—pushed the butch meters to high swagger."

Dhari laughed. "I remember. Rosie's relationship almost ended in divorce. Danny didn't speak to her until New Year's."

"Yeah," Jamie replied at the end of a chuckle, "that would be the one. I don't understand the metamorphosis that allows Rosie to help her move."

"Is Danny there?"

"Oh, yeah. Took the day off work to be here the whole time."

"Well, that explains why you didn't get the messages I left at work."

"Sorry. She has to be out of here today, so I'll have to catch up on today's stuff later." There was a loud noise from the background followed by raucous laughter, then the phone was muffled again. When Jamie returned she was at the end of a hearty laugh. "This should've been on video tape. I cannot describe . . . Rosie just tripped over a box, dropped her end of the mattress and totally flattened Sue beneath it. Sue's screaming under there and Rosie's laughing so hard she can't get up." Jamie burst into another laugh.

Sue is there. Of course she is. Dhari waited for Jamie's attention less patiently this time.

Finally, "Sorry, Dhari. I'm in the other room now. Go

ahead."

"I just had a couple of things I wanted to talk with you about, decisions I have to make here. I wanted your take on it."

"Shoot."

"The realtor came up with an idea—I could divide the land into small parcels, like even as small as an acre, and sell them a little at a time—"

"Why?"

"I'd stand to make a lot more money that way, plus I'd be able to take my time with the house and the stuff in it."

There was no reply from Jamie.

"You still there?"

"Yeah..." Jamie's voice was flat, lacking its natural lift. "What can I tell you that would make any difference right now?"

"I wanted to know what you thought about it."

"It sounds like you're getting plenty of advice where you are."

It was so unusual to find Jamie reacting adversely at all, that Dhari had no ready tools to deal with it. She thought about it for a moment. *What bothers Jamie about this whole thing? Is it my being away, unavailable? Is it her lack of control? But I've tried to include her, make her a part of it. I'm the one who hates anything messing up the status quo.*

"I know this is somewhat of a mess," Dhari began. "I'm really sorry that I couldn't help you today. I'm sure you could have used the help." She waited for words of forgiveness that didn't come. "You want me to sell it all together and just be done with it?"

"I don't know, Dhari. Maybe it isn't any of my concern."

"Of course it is—"

"Not if there is more than friendly advice going on with Erin Hughes."

The remark took Dhari completely by surprise. *She doesn't know about my fantasies. How could she? They are only fantasies. What would make her think...?* "I'm sorry that I've

147

been gone so long, Jamie. I didn't know it was upsetting you like this. As far as Erin goes, she's only been a helpful friend . . . and I haven't kept anything from you, Jamie."

There was no reply from Jamie.

After an uncomfortable pause, Dhari offered, "I don't think this is the best time to talk about it."

Jamie jumped at the offer. "No, it's not. They need me on the other end of a couch right now."

"Will you come down for a couple of days?"

The fact that Jamie hesitated was as much an answer as her reply. "Well, I'll see how work goes."

She knew the decision had already been made, "I'll call you tomorrow night," Dhari promised. "Be careful lifting."

"I will." Her voice returned to a more comfortable tone. "It's these three stooges we have to worry about," she chuckled.

"Okay, I'm sure you'll have stories to tell me tomorrow . . . I hope you will come down. I miss you."

"I miss you, too."

Chapter 24

Dhari had been listening, and even interjected a response now and then, as Erin drove and carried the conversation all the way to Terri Sandler's. Her mind, though, was preoccupied with Jamie. The feeling that lingered since the phone call remained elusive despite her efforts to define it. Was it anger? Not really. How could she be angry with her? Jamie's suspicions weren't any more out of line than her own. Disappointment? Yes, definitely. How often had she asked Jamie to do something just for her? Yet, someone else's needs came before hers. But it's more than disappointment. And it's more than worrying about what Jamie is doing or thinking. It's something bigger than that, something that strikes at the very core of me. Why can't I see it? Why can't I find a clear and reasonable explanation for this uneasiness? Then came her most dreaded worry, gaining a hold as it always did when she felt most vulnerable. Am I slipping, aimlessly wandering near the edge of sanity? Are these feelings a warning sign? Had mother had the same signs and not known what they were? Maybe it is time for therapy. Or, maybe I could block it out, at least for a while, with the best distraction I could find.

~~~~~~~

Dinner proved to be a wonderful part of that distraction. Joyce's culinary skills lived up to every claim. "This is a perfect example," Dhari said as she pushed her chair a little further from the table, "of how too much of a good thing can actually hurt." She frowned and rubbed her stomach. "I've never been so spoiled with food in my life."

Joyce picked up the leftovers. "That's why we look like tudballs," she said, whisking them off to the kitchen.

Terri licked her index finger and marked a score in the air over Dhari's head. "No *carvone* this one," she directed to Erin.

Erin's eyes were on Dhari, as they had been, Dhari realized, all through dinner. The interest seemed more than casual, and was more than welcome. Dhari held her gaze too long this time and Terri noticed.

Dhari quickly diverted her eyes as Joyce called out from the kitchen. "We'll be having wine and conversation in the family room."

Terri rose immediately. "You heard the lady," she said with a nod of her head. "Bring your glasses . . . and yes, you do have room for dessert."

Dhari groaned at the thought of trying to swallow even one more bite, no matter how delicious, but she followed Terri respectfully into the family room.

"How long have you and Joyce been together?" Dhari asked, choosing a chair directly across from Erin.

"On the 4th of July it will be eighteen years. We decided to let the whole country celebrate with us."

The surprise registered on Dhari's face and threw Terri into a full-blown laugh.

"I didn't think anyone stayed together that long anymore," Dhari replied. Except parents who are crazy and don't know any better.

"That's because it takes work," Joyce said as she filled their glasses and joined Terri on the couch. "When the string gets tangled, instead of sitting down and taking the time to straighten it out, they throw it out and start fresh."

"This one's been straightened out so many times it's

beginning to fray," Terri said with a grin.

Joyce cocked her head and looked at her. "Yeah? That's when the ends get dipped in hot wax, Smarty."

Terri winked at Dhari. "Which is why this relationship is working just fine."

"You've got to make a good choice to begin with," Joyce explained, "then be willing to work through the tangles that inevitably occur."

"We are far from the perfect example," Terri added. "We've made as many mistakes as we have good decisions. But we love each other enough to forgive, and accept one another's flaws. When you get a taste of the bad, the good tastes so much sweeter."

The point wasn't missed and Dhari made eye contact with Erin to let her know. Okay, point made. A lesson acknowledged.

Erin, who had been unusually quiet all evening, finally joined the conversation. "How do you know if you're putting the work in on the right relationship, that is, one that has a chance of successfully meeting both your needs?"

"Aw, geez, Doctor," Joyce replied. "You find that answer and you'll be bigger than Dr. Phil."

"The best he's been able to come up with," Terri added, "is 'How's that workin' for ya?' And he's right. Each person has to be able to tell if it's working for them. And the other person, in turn, needs to hear it so that they can act on it together. Otherwise, their individual efforts will be in vain and they'll both be unhappy."

"Happiness is relative, though," Dhari submitted. "It depends on what you know, what you've experienced, and where you want to go in life. How do you know whether you might be happier with someone else?"

Her question was followed by a contemplative silence. Each woman, no doubt, making a quick examination of past choices and ex-lovers. Meantime, Dhari was basking in the heat of Erin's gaze and trying not to look at her.

Terri at least made an attempt at an answer. "I guess it's

that point when you just know, even if you can't explain specifically why, that tells you something magical is going on."

Joyce looked at Terri and nodded. "That's not bad, Honey," she said. "It's a good enough answer for me."

Erin refocused on Terri. "I wish it were good enough for me . . . why do I always have to have everything nailed down, anchored in concrete?"

"You're a historian," Joyce replied. "Validity, authenticity, chronology—you deal in hardened concrete everyday. What do you expect?"

"I have a hard time grasping intangibles," Erin admitted. "I wish I could believe in magic, or at least be able to accept something that I can't quite wrap my mind around. It would save me a lot of frustrating interior dialogue."

And let you believe that your real parents could really have loved you, Dhari thought, instead of spending the rest of your life wondering and searching for proof . . . I wish you could believe, too.

"If it makes you feel any better," Joyce offered, "love isn't something you're ever going to be able to get your mind around. It isn't possible. Poets and philosophers have their go at it, but this is one person who doesn't need to know any more than what's going to keep this lady by my side today."

Erin leaned forward in her chair and rested her forearms on her thighs. "Do you plan for forever? Like did you sit down one day after you got together and decide that you were going to be together for the rest of your life, or did one day just turn into the next until you're here eighteen years later answering questions about how you did it?"

Joyce responded with a short, husky laugh and placed her hand on Terri's thigh. "This one's yours."

The focus was on Terri and a smile that closed her eyes to slits. "Oh, we said things, even early on, like 'I want to grow old with you', 'I never want to be without you'—but there was no real game plan, and if there had been one it would've been obsolete by the following week. We're two different people with different backgrounds, learning and changing at different rates. There isn't much that can be locked in place." She met Joyce's gaze. "Only a commitment to do whatever it takes to make the changes together."

Joyce leaned over and kissed Terri on the lips. "Whatever it takes," she said and smiled.

The questions continued, "Do you think you were destined for each other?" "Is there someone destined for each of us?"

And patiently they were answered, "Oh, yes, definitely destined," and "How else can you account for lovers finding each other after years of choices that have kept them apart?"

All the while the discussion aired around her, Dhari imagined herself sitting on the couch with Erin close beside her. They had made dinner together, sharing the necessary duties, and then talked about their day. Later they would plan a vacation, snuggle together and watch a movie. Maybe they'd make love before they slept, maybe they wouldn't. Maybe they would just hold each other and talk about the movie. One thing she knew for sure, they would wake together in the morning, and all the mornings to come.

"Hey, what do you think, Dhari?"

Dhari broke her stare at the picture of Terri and Joyce that sat on the table next to her and tried to recall the question. "Oh, destiny? I don't know." She noted smiles all around and realized she had lost some time. Her embarrassment was obvious. "I'm sorry," she said, looking from one to another. "It isn't the company, believe me. I'm just having brain farts. What did I miss?"

"The unmasking of love's greatest mysteries," Erin replied.

"According to Atlanta's greatest pseudo intellects," added Joyce.

"Hardly," Dhari returned with a smile. "Can I get the crib notes version?"

"On the way home," Erin promised. "We have to let these two get to bed early. Joyce has to be at work before I'm out of dream state."

"Why don't you let Terri fill her in," Joyce suggested, rising from the couch, "while you help me pack up some leftovers for Jake."

Erin collected the glasses and followed Joyce into the kitchen. "Thank you for another wonderful meal," she said. "And thank you in advance for Jake, he doesn't often get meals like this."

Joyce busily lined up Tupperware, and scooped and topped and bagged leftovers, and all the while she was suspiciously quiet. Finally, she turned and looked full into Erin's eyes. "I think Dhari Weston is a very nice young woman." She watched the expected smile appear on Erin's face, then continued. "And I don't think she has any idea of how badly she could hurt someone . . . but I'm hoping that you do."

Erin's smile dissolved quickly. She said nothing, but did not divert her eyes from Joyce's.

Joyce handed her the grocery bag. "Your interest is pretty obvious, but don't expect us to encourage it. What you can expect is an open door and open arms when hope crashes and burns."

Erin finally broke eye contact. There was nothing she could say. It didn't make sense to argue or offer a feeble denial of awareness. Only a fool denies the obvious.

"I'm not saying that I don't like her, Erin, because I do. I'm concerned about the state of my friend's heart, that's all."

If not for Erin's prodding the trip home might have been made in complete silence.

"Did Terri fill you in on our philosophical meanderings?"

Dhari forced a smile. "Sort of."

"We're not always such eggheads. Joyce and Terri are really a lot of fun."

"Oh, they're wonderful," Dhari remarked. "I felt very comfortable—too comfortable, I guess, or I wouldn't have faded out on you like that." Or daydreamed about something as unrealistic as living with Erin Hughes. The earlier flush that had warmed her from head to toe returned, this time without the impetus of Erin's gaze. *How do I dare even think it? Just because she flirts a little? Because she makes me feel special?*

"They probably assumed, as I did, that you had a lot on your mind." Erin glanced sideways and smiled. "No shame in that. Terri mentioned that you're leaning toward selling the land in small parcels."

"I was."

"That doesn't sound like a lean."

"The idea really upset Jamie. I thought I was the one...I didn't realize how much she needs things to stay the same. She wants me back home."

It took two attempts for Erin to make eye contact. "What does Dhari want?"

Dhari leaned her head back against the headrest and closed her eyes. *What does it matter? When has it ever mattered?* She spoke just above a whisper. "Things that just can't be."

Erin's voice was nearly as soft. "Like what, Dhari?"

The length of the silence caused Erin to take a longer look at Dhari than she should have. She hadn't moved her head from the headrest. A streak of silent tears glistened on her cheek. "Oh, Dhari," Erin said as she reached for her hand.

Immediately Dhari squeezed it and held it tightly as she spoke. "I want my mother not to be crazy...I want Nessie to live forever." She finally turned tear filled eyes to Erin. "See what I mean?"

With her hand still held tightly in Dhari's grasp Erin replied, "We all have wishes that can't be." She turned to face Dhari. "But yours, I must say, are more altruistic than most."

"No," Dhari said with intense seriousness, "they're selfish. Very selfish. I want my family to be happy, to be normal, because I can't fix it and I can't keep trying. And I want Nessie in my life forever because of how she makes me feel, and you and Pip..." she pulled her hand and her eyes from Erin, and left only a narrow profile to which Erin could speak.

"How do we make you feel, Dhari?"

Despite the warmth of the car, Dhari's insides shivered

uncontrollably. She had never intended to say. She had meant to keep what couldn't be to herself. But she hadn't been able to keep anything from this woman yet. "Happy," she said quietly toward the window.

"Hare-hugging-hound, space beneath the soles of your feet?"

A confused Dhari turned quickly from the window to meet Erin's eyes. A spark ignited within her, then immediately turned to fear that that she may be misinterpreting what Erin was saying.

Erin offered a gentle smile. "I'll interpret. Happy enough to hug the hound that's chasing you for his master's dinner—so happy that the thought of me lifts you off the ground? Do I make you that kind of happy?"

She wasn't going to answer that question, at least not until she was sure that she'd gotten it right, but Dhari felt herself nod in affirmation and hold her breath.

"Yes," Erin replied with a directness that made the quivering in Dhari's stomach noticeable once again. "The thought of you lifts me off the ground, Dhari."

The realization sent a bolt of excitement searing through Dhari's chest. She fought for a deep breath and just managed to say, "We shouldn't be having this conversation."

"Another secret you'd rather not know?" Erin asked. When there was no reply, she added, "When I was in the kitchen with Joyce tonight, I was gently warned not to have this conversation."

"So why are we having it?" Dhari asked.

"I can only speak for myself," Erin said, reaching out and taking Dhari's hand again. Dhari did not pull away, and Erin continued. "Even if it doesn't make a difference in whether you stay or not, or whether it changes our lives at all, and I don't expect it to, Dhari, at least I'll never have to wonder 'what if'. I'm not good at wondering."

Erin stopped the truck at the top of the Grayson drive.

"Anchored in concrete," Dhari echoed, looking at their hands. "See, I was listening," she said, her eyes still on their hands as she frantically tried to conjure up rational thoughts to regain control of the wild things happening to her body.

Inviting Erin in probably wasn't the solution she was looking for, but Dhari couldn't help herself. "I don't really want you to leave yet," she said. "Maybe we should talk about this."

Her mind began its rationalization immediately as Erin accepted the invitation and they made their way silently into the house. *This is something else, a different kind of happy, that's all. A friendship,* she continued, sitting next to Erin on the sitting room couch, *a wonderful and important friendship, but just a friendship.*

Nothing, however, was working. The heat generated by Erin's touch grew in the quiet of the house, racing with the beat of her heart to an almost intolerable level. It was exciting and wonderful, and quite possibly more than she could handle. She raised her eyes imploringly to Erin's. What she saw there was making it nearly impossible to say what she should.

Erin made it easy by speaking first. "You don't have to say anything; I don't expect you to. Given the circumstances I don't deserve a response. I may not even deserve the right to tell you what I feel, but . . ." She pulled Dhari into an embrace, held her in her arms as she would hold the most delicate treasure in the palm of her hand.

Dhari pressed against the contour of Erin's body, and felt Erin's lips nuzzling into her hair. *Was it supposed to be this easy? Had it been this easy for Jamie?* There didn't seem to be an answer, and it didn't seem to matter. She touched her lips to Erin's neck and then her cheek. A second later Erin's lips were touching hers—softer than a fantasy, more tender in their touch than the deepest belief. *Oh, I must have wished this—I must have.*

Dhari's hands glided instinctively over the crisp fabric of Erin's shirt, feeling the form of her back, reaching up to let her fingers tease through the soft brown curls covering Erin's neck. Kisses that Dhari had thought hesitant weren't at all.

They were direct against her lips and her face and her neck. They were, Dhari realized, as gentle as Erin's embrace. Yet they were deliberate in their intent, warming her, stirring awake sensations wherever they touched her.

She opened her eyes to Erin's, only briefly, only long enough to see something there that she couldn't identify. Then she parted her lips to a kiss that admitted passion carefully held until now. The edges of thought softened in the tenderness and the heat. The touch of Erin's tongue now, imploring and slow, sent sensations, exquisite sensations, that flooded her consciousness. There was no rush, no friction to ignite the sparks, only the tenderness of touch and a slow deliberate passion that was slowly and wonderfully enveloping her.

Their kisses deepened as Erin's hands began visiting sensitive places, traveling along the length of Dhari's thigh and the curve of her hip. Lips touched the hollow of her neck causing an arousal that rivaled that of the words that had reached within. They whispered now through Dhari's thoughts. 'Space beneath your soles.' 'That kind of happy.' They touched beyond the warmth of her flesh and reached a part of her that had been long ignored, a hunger she had almost forgotten.

Dhari's shirt had been removed with little notice, and her bra lifted carefully over her head. There was no question that Dhari wanted this, no concern for later, only Erin's hands loving her. She let them continue—wanted them to continue—caressing her, loving her, treasuring her.

She lay back against the brocade pillows, under the resolve of Erin's kisses, under her hands, while desire moved quickly from her thoughts to her body. It flowed like blood through her veins—flushing her, heating her, pounding to an ache that grew stronger with every heartbeat.

A low moan escaped her throat as Erin drew down the zipper of Dhari's jeans. Yes, she wanted this, wanted Erin, just this once.

The whispers came again, "I want you to be this happy," breathed hotly now from Erin's lips as they brushed lightly over Dhari's breasts. "As happy as you make me."

A little more time, Dhari pleaded silently as she tried consciously to slow her own responses. This will only happen once, a little more time. It's okay to enjoy it, to savor the slowness, every wonderful moment of it. It's okay.

But Erin's hand, as warm as the flesh it touched, was against her, moving with her, a part of her. Where was she in the wetness, against her, in her? She couldn't tell, but it was wonderful, deep and wonderful. And all she could tell was how near she was, how close, how so few movements away.

Wait. Wait. No, not yet. Dhari pulled her mouth away from the heat of their kiss and clasped her arms tightly around Erin's head and shoulders, quivering in anticipation. This is the moment, the single most perfect moment. Let me hold on to it, she pleaded; let it wrap me in its honesty. Just this once.

But her body would not listen; it exploded in paroxysms of pleasure, cascading from the top of her head to her feet. "Oh, God, Erin. Yes, yes, whatever you're doing, stay right there . . . yes, stay right there."

She clung tightly to Erin while spasm after spasm of pleasure rippled through her. And Erin stayed, moving only when Dhari did, giving her time so still, so intimate, that it seemed Dhari could hear the grateful sigh of her body. Eyes closed, she breathed deep and long and let the scent of Erin Hughes fill her until her body relaxed.

"Shall I hold you for a while?" Erin asked.

Softly Dhari answered, "Yes," and nestled into Erin's embrace. It was a full, strong embrace—comfortable and secure. Dhari wrapped her arms around Erin's waist and rested her head against her chest. She could feel the warmth of Erin's breath in her hair and the steady beating of her heart, and when she heard the words "I love you, Dhari," she let them be.

It wasn't until Erin stirred that Dhari realized that she had fallen asleep. She opened her eyes as Erin kissed her forehead.

"I'm sorry," Erin whispered. "I didn't mean to wake you, but my arm is asleep."

"Oh," Dhari exclaimed, struggling to right herself. She retrieved her shirt from the back of the couch and pulled it over her head.

Erin rubbed her arm until the tingling began to diminish. "Is it a bad sign that we both fell asleep?"

Alert now and clearly aware of the needed response, Dhari began carefully. "Erin, I think I've mislead you. I need to clarify—"

"No, you don't," Erin interjected quickly. "You don't at all." She moved to a less intimate proximity on the couch and continued. "You've been clear from the beginning. I let my feelings . . ." She looked away and shook her head. "Well, my feelings won't even let me apologize. I wanted it to happen, even if it would be the only time."

"It's okay," Dhari replied as she reached for Erin's hand. "I wanted it to happen, too, or it wouldn't have."

Erin raised her eyes to meet Dhari's. "So, now what?"

"We need to draw a friendship line . . . maybe we can find a place, somewhere between sharing secrets and sharing . . . what we just shared." She released Erin's hand. "I've never done this before. I really don't know how to do this."

"It'll be okay," Erin promised. "We'll figure it out." She rose from the couch. "I'd better get home. Jake's probably asleep on the couch again."

Dhari followed her to the door, her own feelings jumbled and spiked with anxiety. "Drive carefully," she managed. "And tell Jake hi," she called before Erin reached the truck. The words all seemed so wrong, so pathetically common and out of place after what had just happened.

Erin returned a nod and a half smile and disappeared into the darkness.

I'm so lame, so obviously adolescent. Dhari shut the front door as the truck lights came on, and tried to imagine how Jamie would sort everything out—neatly, no doubt. Clear from the beginning. No muss, no fuss.

Hands in her pockets, Dhari stood in the middle of the hallway, staring at nothing in particular. The unsettling that plagued her own mind, though, would only allow her to refocus her stare to the computer screen. No sleep tonight, only the language of grants, and figures, and the responsibility of work to structure her thoughts, to give her control. A mental ploy, she realized, much used and often abused, but it relieved the anxiety and that was all that mattered.

Chapter 25

If she thought that merely saying the words was going to safely define her relationship with Erin, Dhari was mistaken. Defining it as a friendship, she found, made her acutely aware of how surely she had crossed that line. Now every thought and every impulse had to be clearly identified, had to fall cleanly on the correct side of the line. Gray areas no longer existed. She knew where the line was now; the task at hand was to keep from crossing it again.

For days she had resisted the impulse to call Erin. Just wanting to talk, just wanting to hear her voice was tiptoeing across the friendship line. And since talking over personal decisions was as well (and discussing them with Jamie was out of the question), she buried them in an obscure part of her brain and returned to the attic to lose herself in the past. That's where she found a clear and legitimate reason to call Erin.

She raced down the stairs, smiling in anticipation, and heard the phone ringing before she reached the downstairs hall.

"Hey," she answered breathlessly, "I was about to call you."

"Perfect," Erin replied. "I've waited to call you because I wanted it to be for the right reason."

"Yes, me too, and it is, a good reason, I mean, I know mine

is, definitely."

Erin laughed on the other end. "And hopefully mine is, too. I assume you'll be seeing Nessie before you leave."

"Of course. Today in fact."

"Would you mind if I go with you? There's something I want to ask her about, and some things that you should hear as well."

"Oh, yes of course. Come out as soon as you can, I have something exciting to show you."

"I'm on my way."

The urge to hug Erin as she walked through the door was redirected toward greeting a talking, wiggling, dancing Pip.

"Oh, yes, I missed you too," Dhari managed between Pip's kisses. "Are you going to go see Nessie with us? We'll go for a walk."

Immediately Pip's ears came up and forward, her eyes stared intently at Dhari's lips for confirmation that she had heard correctly. But before she could say it again, Erin interceded.

"Just a minute, Pip. We'll go in a minute."

The ears relaxed in disappointment and Pip sat down. Her eyes, however, remained on Erin watching for her cue, the magic words.

"First," Erin said with a smile at Dhari, "you have to show me what's so exciting."

"Come on," she said, hustling into the sitting room with Erin and Pip right behind her. She retrieved two small books from the table and handed them to Erin. "These."

Erin flipped anxiously through the first few pages. "Wow, Dhari."

"Yeah," Dhari replied, her face beaming. "Addy's diaries."

"Have you read them?"

"I wanted to wait for you."

"I wouldn't have been so patient in your place." She took Dhari's arm and pulled her to the loveseat. "I can't wait to hear from Addy again."

Once more they were huddled together over the now familiar script and what had become a very personal part of history. And once more Dhari was dealing with what being this close to Erin did to her physically. This time, though, the stirring warmth that enveloped her was under control.

Erin pointed to the date at the top of the page. "This is after Peach Creek," she explained. "After Billy was killed."

"Read out loud," Dhari said, "like you did at Nessie's."

Without hesitation, Erin obliged her.

"'I write this as if it will find its way to you, safe and waiting for me at the end of this ordeal. It is only the worst of my fears that haunts my mind, not what is real. I will push them away and there you will be. Is it possible that you never left Pennsylvania? I see you there with your adored mother, taking good care and writing me of each day's events. And I will read them each night before I sleep, content that you are safe.'"

Erin cleared her throat, strained with emotion, then continued softly.

"'It is not too long to wait; unlike our love, this war will not last forever.'"

She lifted her head and cleared her throat again. "I don't know if I can read this out loud."

"Try," Dhari said. "I like to hear you read. It's as if Addy is saying the words for the first time."

Struggling for composure, Erin began again with the next entry.

"'Although I still expect them, there are no new letters. I read the last of yours over and over to comfort my heart. It is your eyes, sparkling blue, that shine in the darkness of my room before tears of sadness blur my own. I brush them aside to see your face. How strong the lines of your jaw, determined and set in purpose. Could there be any argument that would alter the course of your chosen path? I dare to think it could be made. And if it could, have I failed you, my love? Led you by your love for me to your death? I dare not think it, but rather wait in disavowal for one more look at your face.'"

And then the next excerpt dated August 5, 1864.

"'There is no just and loving God.'"

Erin lifted her head and stared absently across the room.

"That's all she wrote?" Dhari asked.

"Yeah," Erin answered, still staring ahead. "Nothing else on the page." She dropped her eyes to the book.

"It's beginning to sink in—the finality of death."

Erin nodded and read the next page.

"'I cannot bear to go outside, to see again the hill over which I first saw you return. To know again the hope that I felt in my heart at the sight of you. My darling, I could not bear it. What am I to do without you, without hope?'"

And the next.

"'Life has torn from my heart the very thing that living is about. For me to live now is more cruel than all the horrors of this war, but there has been no time for me to die. What greater cause is there to die for than freedom? Only love. While I am honored by such a sacrifice, I am chaffed raw to my very soul by it. For me a life was given. Would there not have been a cause more worthy to live for?

'The only reason I see left for my own life is in the eyes of my precious baby. No innocence is left to me, save in those eyes. They are pure and still untouched by injustice and sorrow. If for no other purpose I choose to live to give her the hope that I have lost.'"

"Okay, now I can't go any further," Dhari said, shifting uneasily. "Let's go to Nessie's, and maybe read more later."

"It accumulates, doesn't it? Grief." Erin closed the diary but did not lift her eyes. "Even reading about it, it accumulates . . . Yes, let's go to Nessie's."

Pip bounded along the path ahead of them as if she knew where she was going. For her it was an adventure. For her companions, it was a therapeutic walk in fresh air to help dilute the potency of their emotions. And it worked. Pip monopolized their attention, darting into the tall grasses at sounds and smells that were indiscernible by Dhari and Erin, barking, rustling and always finding her way back to the path. She bounced in circles and danced on her hind legs, totally frustrated that her best efforts were unsuccessful in convincing her humans to follow her into the wilderness on an exciting mystery chase.

By the time they reached Nessie's, uncomfortable emotions and unprocessed thoughts had been dropped along the side of the path. Both women were smiling and Pip was panting when Nessie greeted them at the kitchen door.

"Sunshine," Dhari said as she handed Nessie a bouquet of early yellow tulips.

"And sweets," Erin added with a Tupperware of pancake size sugar cookies.

Nessie giggled as Pip brushed between her ankles and began investigating the corners and crevices of the kitchen. The women bustled about the little kitchen readying the table with flowers and snacks. It gave Dhari a great feeling of familiarity and quiet comfort . . . she had the whole rest of the day to enjoy it. There would be no thought of tomorrow and leaving. No sad feelings of missing what had become so unexpected a joy in her life. There would be plenty of time for that later. For now, she was not going to allow anything to diminish the happiness that she felt. She smiled easily and relaxed in a chair next to Erin.

Pip had finally settled in Erin's lap, evidently content that any rodent problem must be under control. Dhari studied the little black face. Such sweetness, she thought, in those round dark eyes. Whatever else might be there, the forgiving sweetness is what shines through. Dhari switched her focus to the tiny woman sitting across from her. What pain there must be buried beneath the sweetness in those eyes?

These are faces I'll see in my mind for the rest of my life—and Erin's—how quietly and clearly it has become a part of every day. And there it will stay. No one needs to know. It will be a secret comfort only for me.

"Now Jake," Erin was explaining as Nessie broke her sugar cookie in half, "has to add about a quarter of an inch of peanut butter on the top." She shook her head. "I envision peanut butter lining the walls of his arteries, so I left him only a couple."

"Yer a good daughter," Nessie said crunching her cookie.

"He's a good father. I can't imagine life without him." Erin dunked a piece of cookie in her glass of milk. "Which brings me to something I wanted to talk about, Nessie. Well, first, Dhari found Addy's diaries and we read the entries right after Billy's death. Her loss was so apparent—"

"And hard to read about," Dhari added.

Nessie leaned forward and spoke softly. "It's good souls dat can catch da spirit of someone else's grief, 'specially when ya can't see dere tears."

"But you can feel them in her words," Erin replied. "She was devastated. If it wasn't for her baby, I wonder if she would've ended her own life."

Nessie shook her head. "Not Grandma Addy. Never dat. My momma used to say she had a will even Sherman couldn't break . . . Don't know why dem genes didn't pass on to Miss Mary."

Erin's expression was pensive. "Genetics will always be a mystery, I'm afraid."

Dhari reached for another cookie and broke it in half. She guessed that Erin's discomfort had mostly to do with not knowing her own genetics, but she wondered if there was something else she was missing. She decided to ask Erin later.

"Ever wonder how dat house survived Sherman's plan?" Nessie asked.

Erin smiled. "That's one of the things that I wanted to ask you about. I thought there might have been more to that story than you told me."

And a lot more to it than I know, Dhari concluded.

"Da slave houses was all burned so's dey'd leave. How else ya free da slaves?"

"And the livestock and fields and everything else was

destroyed to make the southern citizens feel that the consequences of war were so horrible that they would never want another," Erin added.

"Da slaves wrapped and buried food in secret places so's da soldiers couldn't steal it, and dat dere would be food enough to get da families by after da army left." Nessie's eyes were fixed and intense, the family elder with her young charges anxiously gathered around her. "Da big house was still standin' and when da soldiers came to search it, Miss Addy met dem at da door. She had baby Mary in her arms and da lieutenant told her to grab whatever personal belongings she could carry and leave da house. He sent his soldiers to look for food and jewelry."

Neither Erin nor Dhari moved as they waited for Nessie to take a drink of milk and continue.

"Miss Addy handed Mary to Talitha, da foreman's wife, and told her to take her somewhere safe, den she stood her ground. She said 'You look in dis face. Do you see your wife here, or could it be a sister or mother you see in dese eyes? Would you leave dem in such despair? You can't see what your war has taken from me, my father, my husband, my reason for life.' Den she pulled dat ole rocker dat still sits by da window into da hallway and sat down. 'Dis house,' she told him, 'is all I have left to give my baby. If you must burn it, you will do so wid me in it.'"

"And it worked," Dhari exclaimed with a huge smile.

"It surely did," Nessie said. "Dat lieutenant took off his cap and nodded his respect and went on his way."

"And she went on," Erin added. "Running her farm, raising her daughter, living her life."

"Surely did," Nessie nodded. "Surely did."

The sun began its descent on the walk home, a blazing orange ball sinking slowly behind the tall grass. When they reached the big house the sky had changed into ribbons of orange and pink, a brilliant backdrop to the old beech tree.

Dhari and Erin settled on the wooden bench and watched silently as the colors merged and faded into pastel.

"So, finish telling me about Mary," Dhari said.

Erin picked up Pip and placed her on Dhari's lap. "That's partly why I called. When I talked with Nessie earlier today she started telling me about Anna and Emily. Nessie and your aunt and grandmother were quite young when Mary killed herself. That's what Nessie was referring to when she said that she didn't know why Mary hadn't inherited Addy's genes, her strength of spirit."

The initial shock must not have registered on Dhari's face since Erin made no indication that her information had been disturbing. Years of experience, Dhari thought, of keeping my private fears private.

Her silence didn't seem to tip Erin off either. Erin continued. "From what Nessie says, Mary's death was partly what sent your grandmother Emily packing. She was never able to accept Addy as a parent, and she and Anna didn't get along. If Anna liked something, Emily automatically hated it. It sounded like Emily was contrary to things just to be contrary—as if she didn't know where to place the blame for her mother's death, so she put it on everyone and everything. It seems Anna was the one to inherit Addy's spirit. She was a feminist by nature—went to the high school ball unescorted, later marched with Dr. Martin Luther King in Selma, and campaigned as tirelessly for the ERA as Addy had for the vote. Emily, on the other hand, ran away with some boy to Indiana and eventually married a Methodist minister. Their lives couldn't have been more different."

Dhari seemed deep in thought, fingers absently stroking the little dog's head. Erin tapped her finger gently to Dhari's temple. "Let me in?" she asked.

Dhari smiled. "I'm doing it again, fading; but I heard what you were saying . . . I was just thinking about how some genes seem to skip generations."

Erin nodded. "I've heard about studies that support the theory in some cases, but I don't remember the specifics."

"It doesn't matter. Even if there is one that includes mental illness, I wouldn't trust it . . . Remember when I said turning you away was the most unselfish thing I've done?"

"I hope you're about to tell me why."

"If you could see what my mother's illness has done to our family, to my father . . . I made a conscious decision that I would never do that to anyone. And I won't. Jamie Bridgewater will never allow me to. She'll protect herself above all else—she'll leave." Dhari looked into the dark blue eyes that she knew would haunt her dreams for years to come. "But, you," Dhari said, locking into the blueness, "would stay."

"Are you willing to live your whole life in preparation for something that may never happen?" Erin asked. "You would deny yourself years of joy and happiness out of fear?"

Dhari dropped her eyes. "I do have happiness with Jamie. And part of that happiness is not worrying about hurting her."

"Hurt can happen in other ways, Dhari. There are no safe guards. Maybe leaving you would hurt her more than you think."

"But it would be nothing compared to staying with someone who is mentally ill—when drugs don't work, and their side effects make you miserable or make you stop taking them all together, and your illness becomes the focus of your life, and love and happiness are of little consequence to you. No, Jamie won't allow it; I'm counting on that."

"And what if you're wasting your life focusing on an illness that you'll never even have? You don't just shortchange yourself, you shortchange everyone around you. They're left with a part-time friend, a less-than-committed lover. Think about it," Erin said, "Maybe they'd rather have all of you, flawed and imperfect, just as you are—just as we all are."

"I wish I could believe that," Dhari said softly. Oh, God, how I want to believe that. "I know you believe it."

"I didn't always. I had to have proof that I could be loved just as I am; I needed proof. I must have been given away because I was flawed, I reasoned. So, what do my adoptive parents mean when they say that they love me? How could they? Soon they'd see the flaws and know why I was given away, and they would give me up, too. I waited, I watched for a sign—after I broke my mother's prized vase, after I lost the twenty dollars Dad gave me to buy a present for Mom, after the 'D' in algebra. But there were no conditions that I had to meet for their love—it was there, time and time again, stronger than ever. That's when I knew; that's when I believed." Dhari's eyes, large and brown and doubtful, stared into her own. "I don't know what's out there for me; I have no idea what I may find out about myself—I could be the result of a rape, of incest, I could be bi-racial. Something like that could have had consequences for me. Would that change what you thought of me?"

"Of course not."

Erin pushed back a wayward sprig of Dhari's hair and cupped her cheek in her hand. "Then know one thing, Dhari, before you leave; you are loved for who you are. I love you for who you are."

Dhari covered Erin's hand with her own and closed her eyes. She felt wonderful—warm and safe and tingling with excitement. For the moment, she could think of nothing except how much she wanted Erin to kiss her. Then, as if she had said the words aloud, Erin's lips were on hers, and they were warm and tender and lovely.

All that mattered right now was Erin's arms around her, Erin's lips moving over her face and neck, and being here. Nothing else was allowed to intrude—no worry, no guilt—nothing to spoil this pleasure.

She let her arms circle Erin's waist, allowed her lips to search out Erin's, gave herself permission to feel the love being offered one more time. It made her heart skip and run like an excited child. Her lips gave in to Erin's gentle insistence, parting and welcoming their pressure. She was being enveloped, mind and body, in a spiral of warmth. The pull of it was irresistible and overwhelming.

"I do love you, Dhari," Erin breathed against parted lips.

"Forgive me but I can't help it."

Dhari pressed harder into a kiss, fighting a sudden rush of resistance. She pulled Erin into a tighter embrace and kissed her again. The intensity of it ebbed and flowed until Dhari separated them enough to whisper, "Tell me that you would leave—that you would never let me hurt you." She touched Erin's lips tenderly again. "Tell me."

Erin pressed her forehead against Dhari's and spoke softly. "I can't." She felt Dhari loosen her embrace. "If this love is what I think it is, Dhari, I could never leave you."

"And I could never risk hurting you."

They held each other for a long time, there under the witness tree, letting the emotion between them ebb, knowing that this would be goodbye.

Dhari finally broke the silence. "Will you keep the diaries for me?" she asked, retreating from Erin's arms.

Erin took a deep breath and leaned back against the bench. "You're not curious?"

Dhari nodded, but did not make eye contact. "I have too much to deal with when I get home." She chanced a look into Erin's eyes. "And I know you want to finish them . . . Promise that you will call me and tell me what you find?"

"I'll call," Erin said with a frown. "Promise me that you'll listen to your heroine."

Dhari gave her a questioning look.

"Miss Eleanor was speaking to you when she said 'It is better to light a candle than to curse the darkness' . . . Light your candle, Dhari. Illuminate the corners that you're so afraid to look into."

"As soon as I figure out how."

Chapter 26

The increased pressure imposed by coming back home was no surprise to Dhari, but she had not expected the overwhelming impact it would have on her decisions.

Although she'd met all her deadlines for work, coming back to the office brought her impending decision about accepting the promotion front and center. Rich Avery's memo welcoming her back was accompanied by another copy of the new job description. Implicit in all discussions with Erik was the underlying assumption that once Dhari applied, Rick would offer her the job, and she would accept the promotion. And, although subtle, the same assumptions seemed to be held by her co-workers. All making it very apparent that for two weeks she had not given the decision serious thought. The best she could do now was be grateful for Rick's patience and understanding and take the additional time he offered to make her decision. Why the decision needed much thought was beyond even Dhari, but it just wasn't a decision she was ready to make.

What she had been giving a lot of thought, and phone time, was how to convince her siblings to put aside their personal issues and come together to help their mother celebrate her birthday. Guilt had to be induced carefully and subtly, promises for a happy and rewarding day had to be made clear and often. The phone had become a permanent part of her anatomy. Her monthly minutes had nearly reached their limit in one week's time. But she felt that if all went smoothly it would have been well worth all her efforts.

Somehow the birthday plans had been successfully woven into Jamie's already time constraining agenda of pool at the Aút Bar, and Chinese dinner, and nights of cards and movies and the like. That had all been exhausting enough, but Saturday at the zoo with Jamie and her nephews amounted to Webster's definition of masochism without the sexual gratification.

Ordinarily, today's activity would have been at the top of her chosen to-dos with Jamie, but it came at the end of the wrong week. A demanding week without the soothing sound of Erin's voice, without the comfort of her nearness, and the special balance she created for Dhari. Many times during the day she found herself longing for the less demanding days at the Grayson house. She reminded herself, however, that every week wasn't going to be this heavy. Take one thing at a time, she exhorted herself, concentrate on it. Don't let your mind flutter. All will get taken care of one at a time…with or without Erin.

It hadn't escaped her that Jamie's mind, too, had been troubled. Ever since this whole thing with the house and property had begun there had been indications that Jamie had sensed changes that she wasn't comfortable with. As Dhari's interest in the house had increased, so had Jamie's suspicions that the interest involved more than the house and family history—even before Dhari realized it. They only spoke of it once. A quick admission on Dhari's part, difficult and necessary, a quiet acknowledgement from Jamie. And then, Jamie's way of competing, filling every minute possible with activity, leaving very little time for discussion.

~~~~~~~

With a long groan Dhari collapsed onto the couch.

"I'll ditto that," Jamie groaned, entering the room and dropping down next to her. "This is probably the wrong time to mention taking the boys to Cedar Point."

Dhari closed her eyes with another groan. "It's not open for the season, yet," she replied. "Thank God."

Jamie laughed and gratefully kissed her on the cheek. "Thank you. You've been great."

Dhari turned her head against the back of the couch and met Jamie's eyes. "Am I?" she asked. "I don't feel so great."

"Why Dhari? What's wrong?"

Dhari shrugged her shoulders. "Nothing. Everything. I don't know." The space between her brows narrowing into two small creases, she asked, "What do you see when you look at me? Who am I to you?"

Jamie replied, almost offhandedly, "You're my lover," but her expression questioned why a reply was even necessary.

"Is that all?"

"Where's this going, Dhari?"

"A place we haven't gone before," she persisted, noting Jamie's frown, a rare but recognizable sign of discomfort. A sign that had successfully derailed the questions which Jamie's mother raised about girlfriends; the same one that had always warned friends that they were about to trespass, and halted them abruptly in their tracks. Yet Dhari trod on.

"What kind of person am I? Am I an honest person? A giving person? If I was grilling steak and I dropped one on the floor and washed it off and cooked it, would you say I'd secretly give it to you, or would I eat it myself? Do you know that the smell of roses makes me nauseous?"

Jamie seemed stunned, staring at Dhari as if attempting to answer might touch off another run of questions.

Dhari waited.

Finally, when it was apparent that only a reply would ease the tension, Jamie said, "I'm a pretty good judge of character, Dhari. I wouldn't enter a remake of the Newly Wed Game—that flower thing threw me—but I think I know you."

Dhari shook her head. "You've never needed to know anymore about me than was apparent—that I love being with you, that I accept your friends, that I understand your family situation. And that was okay with me, too. At least I thought it was. But it really isn't, it isn't okay any longer."

"What are you saying? I don't understand. This is because I didn't come down to Atlanta, isn't it?"

"It isn't about you at all, Jamie. It's about me trying to recognize what I need and being able to articulate that. I've been a hypocrite thinking that I could help fix other people's lives when I can't even define my own."

Dhari sat up and faced Jamie, who by not responding hoped that the matter might subside. But Dhari pressed on. "At first I thought you needed me to help you find a way to reconcile with your family, that I would be a meaningful part of that process. But when I watched you creating diversions and surrounding yourself with people to fill the different needs in your life, I found myself envying you for being able to do that on your own."

"No, don't envy me. I'm just an exercise in evolution, a primitive creature, adapting to my environment for survival. In the process I've learned that there are very few things we really need in life—food, shelter, love—you get those where you can and poke fun at the rest." Jamie raised her arms as if they were giant wings, "Less wear and tear on the Pterodactyl wings, that way, when you stay above the trees."

"I wish it were that simple for me," Dhari sighed. "There are things I have to know about myself, decisions I have to make. We need to talk about—"

Jamie interrupted, taking Dhari's hand and pulling her down into an embrace. She whispered in Dhari's ear, "Who says it can't be simple? Some things are very simple," she said, pressing her lips into the warmth of Dhari's neck. "This is definitely one of them," she murmured. "Simple . . . clear," she breathed, touching Dhari's lips gently at first, then harder as Dhari began to respond.

It's true. Simple, this need I feel. Clear. This is what I need, what I want, Jamie to keep away the craziness, to make it easy, difficult to acknowledge the demons.

She moaned heated encouragement to Jamie's kisses, ready to let her body make its own decisions. Ready for the heat to burn away the worry. No thought, no worry, no decision, no fear. Let her hands go where they know to go, do what they know to do. They'll find the places, touch them and bare them, and ravish them with want. My heart will race until my breath comes short, and desire taking the helm will chart its own course.

Jamie knew where to tease, running her fingers lightly inside the edge of Dhari's bra, caressing her breast while the heat of her mouth seared through the fabric over her breast. The response was almost always immediate, always the same—moans of pleasure followed by grasping Jamie's head and arching upward pressing into Jamie's mouth. Signals Jamie knew well, compelling flesh on flesh. Flushed and ready, Dhari's body responded as usual with urgency to Jamie's mouth caressing the well-known path downward. Her hands tugged insistently the zipper of Dhari's jeans. She could always take her there so quickly, to that place where she controlled the uncontrollable and brought pleasure immeasurable . . . just as she had all week. But something was different today. Dhari's hands held, but didn't grasp. Her body warmed, but remained still. Jamie pulled back and circling her arms around Dhari, buried her face against Dhari's shoulder. She held her tightly. Nothing was said for a long moment.

Dhari gently caressed the back of Jamie's head. "I'm sorry," she whispered.

"Are you worried about tomorrow, your mom's birthday thing?"

"Tomorrows," Dhari replied, disregarding that Jamie usually was reluctant to talk about such things.

Jamie lifted her head and softened her embrace, allowing Dhari to nestle against her. She didn't say anything, but at least made no indication that she would walk away from the conversation.

"Being with you," Dhari continued, "usually keeps those kind of worries at bay."

"Tomorrow's going to be fine," Jamie assured. "And if it's not, you'll deal with it then. Worrying about all the 'ifs' that may never happen will just make you crazy."

The unfortunate reference sent an immediate chill over Dhari, raising the hairs on her skin. She knew it was an innocent reference and let it pass. "If-dog-rabbit," Dhari said.

Jamie looked puzzled.

"It means the same thing as worrying about the 'ifs' that may never come," Dhari explained. "A saying from Jacob Hughes's *The South as I Say It* ... Jake is Erin's father, a colorful and wise old southern gentleman."

"Mm," Jamie mused.

"Part of what I've been trying to tell you, Jamie, is that I'm not you. So much in my life as I was growing up was unpredictable, uncontrollable. I try now to foresee what might happen in the future so that I have a chance of influencing it into something I want, or at least can accept. But then I come face to face with possibilities so scary that I run from them."

"It never occurred to me," Jamie said, "that what works for me might not work for you ... I haven't even asked you what you really need, have I?"

"Until recently I couldn't have told you if you'd asked ... Maybe I'm growing up," Dhari replied.

"So, what do you need, Dhari Weston?"

"I need grounding," she answered, sitting up and out of Jamie's embrace. "Something solid that I can count on always being there; something special that is uniquely mine. I don't understand it all yet, but I'm recognizing differences in how I feel emotionally. Things matter to me that never have before." Her voice had a quality of quiet excitement. "I didn't know why I couldn't just sell that house, why I couldn't just walk away without thinking that I might regret it. The decision to sell seemed so final, like something important to me would be lost forever. As a result, I'm in a kind of limbo and can't bring myself to let it go."

Jamie cocked her head as if she were seeing Dhari for the first time. She said nothing, just listened.

"I think what I'm trying to do is make everything fit together—the new feelings and old—and I don't know where the line is, the one between selfishness and self-need."

"You're going to have to explain that better," Jamie said.

"What if I said that I wanted to move to Atlanta," she said, eyes boring hard into Jamie's, "and I wanted you to go with me? Wouldn't that be a selfish thing to want?"

Jamie's eyes dropped away. She leaned heavily against the arm of the couch and offered no reply.

"See? It would be selfish. I can't ask that."

"But you want to," Jamie said, rising from the couch. "You want me to say that I'll make the sacrifices for you—to leave my friends, to start a business all over again, yet you've never said it, Dhari. You've never said 'because I love you, I want to spend the rest of my life with you.'" She turned her back and paced the length of the room. "Neither of us has," She realized aloud.

Jamie turned back toward Dhari who hadn't moved from the couch. "I thought we both felt the same way about that—that the relationship would just naturally go there if it was meant to . . . Are you saying that for you it has gone there, that you want us to make that commitment? Because I don't know if I can, Dhari. I'm not saying I can't, I just don't know if I can."

"See, that's what I don't know, either. Things are changing for me, and I can't seem to stop them. I don't even know if I would stop them if I could because they feel so right for me. But is it unfair of me to expect you to accept those changes?"

"I like things the way they are, or were, Dhari. Maybe I'm too primitive a creature to adapt any further, but I'm not willing to uproot everything that works in my life to go down there and risk you falling in love with Erin Hughes."

"I said goodbye to her, Jamie. I left it as a friendship."

Jamie moved closer to stand in front of Dhari who still had not moved. "Because you're also afraid of risk?" She met Dhari's uplifted eyes. "I'm sorry that I'm not going to be able to make this easy for you. But I only know one thing for sure, if you can't be happy here with me, then you won't be happy there with me, either," she said, her hands spread to her sides. "This has to be your decision, Dhari, and yours alone."

Dhari sprang to her feet and flung herself into Jamie's arms. "No," she said, burying her face against the collar of Jamie's shirt. "I can't make that decision."

"Yes, you can," she replied, holding Dhari tightly, "sooner or later. Just be absolutely sure when you do."

Chapter 27

How she had managed to talk them all into celebrating her mother's birthday, Dhari couldn't say, but all Lela's children and grandchildren were there. The fact that most of them had missed Thanksgiving and Christmas and Easter probably accounted for enough guilt to give a fairly large nudge, so Dhari had no delusions that it was all her own doing. But she felt good about it anyway.

The preparation work had begun hours before—food and drink and cake and wrapped presents. No surprises, except for what was wrapped. Lela hated surprises, and none of her buttons were to be left uncovered. Everything was in the basement, tables set up, snacks and drinks arranged. Dhari's old bedroom had become a little game room, ready with videos for the kids and space for them to play with their toys behind a closed door. The timing was well thought out; give grandma kisses and birthday wishes, watch her open presents, then take all food items in the game room with Aunt 'future elementary teacher' Deanne supervising. Perfect.

The sign on the side door reminded everyone that only Dhari and her father were allowed upstairs, the area most favored by Lela's compulsions. She had tried to think of everything. It was important that after a year and a half of division and separation that this gathering go smoothly. And as usual, Dhari had been vigilant from the moment the first sibling walked in the door.

Douglas grabbed a five-year-old nephew off the basement stairs, tossed him up onto his shoulder and tickled him all the way back to the game room.

"Thank you," Dhari said as Douglas emerged from the room and closed the door behind him.

"I can't believe you pulled this off," he said. "Look at her over there." He motioned toward Lela sitting at the table between Donna and Dana. "Smiling and acting all happy. Who'd ever guess she's a Looney Tune?"

"Don't call her that, Doug. Just keep in mind how quickly things can change. I'll need your help until everyone leaves."

He raised his open hand shoulder high and waited for Dhari to grasp it. "Okay, I'm off for another piece of cake."

The rest of the men had congregated in the TV corner to watch the game. Dhari joined her sisters and her mother at the table where the conversation sounded much like a Truth or Dare game.

Dana was directing her comments and quite a smug look at Donna. "Well, what about the time you had three dates, Miss Too Good, on the same day? And don't act all confused. You knew exactly what you were doing—making me lie to poor Jimmy Buckner and tell him that the car that just drove up was my date. Rushing him out the door after he had gotten you flowers and a Valentine's card."

Donna flushed and straightened in her chair. "I was young. No one told me that that's not how you play the field."

Lela looked somewhat perplexed. "There are so many things that I don't know about my own children."

"That's okay, Mom," Dhari interjected. "Wouldn't you rather just think that Donna was always a good little girl?"

Donna made a face at Dhari that pushed the boundaries of charitable demeanor. Dhari just smiled in return.

"I can't believe Jimmy is dead," Dana said matter-of-factly. "I guess when you're young you don't think of people your age dying."

The news obviously surprised Donna. "I didn't know he died. What happened?"

"Brain aneurysm," Dana replied. "He was twenty-eight. Had a headache one day and was gone the next. But what was weird? His mother died of the same thing at the same age. Now, some doctor should have seen that coming."

The information was old news, but it was still disturbing. It sent Dhari's thought immediately to Erin. *Of course she needs to know who her parents are—or were. Knowing is not only an emotional need. How stupid of me not to understand how important it is. All I could think about was how much I didn't want to know my own genealogy. God, how could she fall in love with someone so thoughtless? There has to be a way for her to find out. There must be something she hasn't tried. I wasn't even thoughtful enough to ask. I have to call her. There must be something we can do.*

Lela's voice interrupted Dhari's thoughts. It had a slight edge to it. "Dhari, where's your father?"

"Oh, I don't know, Mom," she said, looking quickly at the TV corner where only one sleeping brother-in-law remained. "Sit tight, I'll go get him. Is there something I can get you?"

"No, I wanted to ask him something, that's all."

Dhari was up immediately. "I'll be right back."

She scanned the basement, then bound up the stairs two at a time, nearly running into Douglas as he came in the door.

"Where's Dad?" she asked anxiously.

"Took Jeff to the store, why?"

"Aw, damn, Douglas. You should've taken him. Why didn't you go?"

"Everything is fine. He won't be gone long."

"Dhari?" Lela called from the bottom of the stairs. "Did you find him?"

"Yeah, Mom," she said, giving her brother a discerning look with which he was all too familiar. One of Lela's buttons was about to rear its ugly head.

Lela met them at the top of the stairs and there was no way around it.

"Hey, Mom," Douglas said as upbeat as he could manage. "Dad took Jeff to the store. He'll be right back."

Lela's face drooped immediately, her balance wavered and she had to grab the handrail to steady herself.

"Come on, Mom," Dhari said, taking her arm. "We'll wait for him in the living room." Then she turned to Douglas and whispered. "Time for everyone to go home. Mom's tired."

He nodded and headed for the basement.

"How can he do this to me?" Lela mumbled. "It's my birthday, how could he do this today?"

"He drove Jeff to the store, that's all. You know Dad, he won't let anyone drive if he's been drinking. I'm sure Jeff wanted more beer. It's my fault. I thought that by not having much on hand he wouldn't drink so much."

"He had to ruin my birthday," Lela continued, dropping heavily onto the couch, "like he's ruined my life. I know where's he's going."

"To the store, Mom." Dhari sat next to her mother. "Please don't get down, it's your day today. Everyone was here so that you'd have a wonderful birthday. And they all had a good time."

"You don't know," Lela said, sounding as if she were about to cry. "You don't. Nobody knows."

"Here, Mom, lie down and rest. It's been a long day. I'm tired, too. I'll be back in a few minutes and we'll talk. I'm going to go down and help clean up and say good-bye, okay?"

She settled her mother on the couch and hurried downstairs.

Lela lifted her head from the couch pillow but didn't bother to wipe the wetness from her face. "What does she look like?" she muttered as she slowly sat up. "Why don't I know what she looks like?"

She stared straight ahead for a few moments until she realized that she was staring at Dhari's backpack that was leaning against the chair. "I'll know who she is before I die." She rose from the couch and unhooked the keys from the zipper of the backpack. "I'll know who it is who sent me to my grave."

Lela let herself out the side door, past the voices coming from the basement and past a grandson bouncing a ball in the driveway.

"Where ya going Grandma?" he asked, but received only a pat on the head as Lela passed.

Without notice she slipped into Dhari's car, which was parked in front of the neighbor's house and pulled away. "You think I'll never find you, but you're wrong. I will. I won't rest until I do."

She drove through the neighborhood and past the school grounds, repeating her promise over and over. Worrying and questioning, and damning Don for her imagined betrayal, Lela drove her daughter's car out of the residential area and into town.

"Where are you? Where are you?" she repeated again and again, tears streaming down her cheeks. She gripped the wheel tighter and tighter as she drove aimlessly from one part of town to another. She saw a number of parking lots but never entered them to search for Don's car. Her course became increasingly more erratic as she struggled to bring the unknown woman's face into focus.

"Why, Don, why?" she implored as she approached the same intersection for the third time.

The 'whys' were lost in the sudden scream of brakes and the deafening explosion that followed, plunging Lela's world into darkness.

Dhari checked the bedrooms and the bathroom again as she returned down the hallway. Once more through the living room, and then she headed for the basement stairs.

"Douglas," she called from the top, her concern growing. "Have you seen Mom?"

Douglas appeared quickly. "No," he called up to her. "She's not down here. What's wrong?"

Before she could answer, her father opened the side door: "Hey, where is everyone? Dhari, I thought you had left; I don't see your car out here anywhere."

"Oh great!" She pushed past Jeff and her father and ran to the front of the house where she threw her arms in the air at the empty space where her car had been.

Her father's concern was obvious. "What is it, Dhari?"

Exasperated, she replied, "Mom."

"Looking for me?" he asked, his brow furrowing.

"That's my best guess. She's in a bad funk."

"I should've know better," he said pressing his fingers hard into his temple. "She seemed so good today, though."

"Do we wait, Dad, or do we go look for her?"

The side door burst open with a loud bang, and Douglas rushed out. "Everyone in my car." He shouted. "There's been an accident."

Chapter 28

Everyone's attention turned immediately to the emergency room doctor as he entered the waiting area.

"Donald Weston?"

"Yes," Don replied, jumping to his feet. "How is she? Is she going to be all right?"

Dhari and Douglas rose to join their father.

"She's conscious," the doctor began, "but understandably in a state of shock. She's not going to be making much sense right now, but I want to hold off on a sedative until we can determine the extent of her injuries. The preliminary tests show a number of fractures—her left arm and leg and two ribs. But the head injury is the one we need a good look at."

"Can we see her?" Dhari asked.

"I'm going to let you see her in about an hour. So, try to make yourselves as comfortable as you can. There's coffee and vending machines down the hall there. The cafeteria is on the second floor." He offered his hand to Don and added, "I'll be back out to talk with you as soon as I can."

"Wait, doctor," Don said as he released his hand. "The woman in the other car, how is she?"

"Bruised from the airbag. A broken nose. But she's going to be okay."

"I feel terrible. It wasn't her fault. The police said that my wife never stopped at the stop sign."

"She's going to be fine. You folks try to relax now."

Relax. Maybe a little. Lela was alive, injuries to others at a minimum, and the RAV was fully insured. Dhari finally let go of the death-grip she had on Douglas' hand.

Douglas in turn addressed Dana who had been uncharacteristically quiet since they had arrived at the hospital. "Why don't I take you and Eric home? We can call the rest of the family and fill them in, and Dhari can call us after they talk to the doctor."

It was all the reason Dana needed. She nodded, patted her dad's arm, and followed the men to the car.

Dhari pulled her dad back to a seat, and brought him a cup of coffee. But, despite the relatively good news, there didn't seem to be a noticeable change is his distress level. He rose and paced, and sat, and rose and paced again.

"I know waiting is hard, Dad, but I think she's going to be okay. Sit and talk to me, it'll help."

He obliged her by returning to his seat, but remained silent.

"Would you feel better if Douglas were here? He'll come right back if I call him."

"No, Honey," he replied. "That's not necessary."

"I'm sorry, Dad, this is all my fault. Why do I think I can fix everything? Why can't I just leave things alone?" Her eyes began to water but she wiped them quickly and clenched her jaw. She took a deep breath before continuing. "You and Mom would have been fine if I'd just stayed out of it."

"No, it's not your fault," he said. "And it's not your mother's fault." He leaned forward, elbows to knees, and rested his head in his hands. "How could she have known? There was no way she could have known."

"Dad, what are you talking about?"

"What have I done?" He cried into his hands. "What have I done?"

How could she have known? Dhari looked at her father. He was falling right before her eyes; he was confessing. Dhari closed her eyes. I don't want to hear this. Please don't let this be true.

"You don't have to tell me this," she whispered close to his head. "We'll get her help now, she'll be okay."

He raised his head. Eyes red and blurred with tears looked into his daughter's. "I would have lost her, would've lost my babies," he said, gently touching Dhari's cheek. "You would have grown up hating me."

What do you say to a fear with such validity? Lying, cheating, divorce—a mother devastated and alone. Of course we could have hated him. And letting him think otherwise would only elevate the guilt of a bad decision to unbearable levels. There was nothing to say. She would comfort him if she could, wouldn't she?

"When?" she asked softly.

"A long time ago," he said, his eyes distant and sad.

The deduction came easily. "Before we moved."

"She was a grad assistant. She was going to travel and teach in different parts of the world. I was still young enough—dreams still clear enough—still possible." He was staring, unfocused, absently turning the wedding band around his finger. "I was wrong. So terribly wrong."

"Was she the only one?"

He nodded. "But there may as well have been fifty . . . whatever problems your mother might have had, I must have magnified them a hundred fold."

Wasn't this just the kind of thing she had hoped to hear over the years? Validation for her mother's suspicions, for her anger? Something that would relieve her own fears and give her hope. She never expected that actually hearing it would make her feel so lousy.

"Mr. Weston?" the doctor said. "You can come in now. I'll ask you to keep your visits short, though, for today."

Dhari waited until they were just outside the room before saying anything. "Dad, I'm only going to stay for a few minutes, then I'll go call Douglas. I think you need the time alone with Mom. Please, though, as much as you may be tempted to get it all said, now is not the time to confess to Mom. We need to get her better first."

Dhari dropped back into the front seat of Douglas's car. "Somebody will be pulling the loaner car around front in a few minutes. These guys think that the insurance company will total out the car. I expected it anyway. Looks like I'll be car shopping again."

"Yeah, I'll go with you," he said absently. Then suddenly Douglas slammed the palm of his hand against the top of the steering wheel. "Does he even care what he's done to this family?"

"He cared about losing his wife," Dhari said. "He cared that his children would grow up hating him."

"So for all his 'caring' we grow up all fucked up, embarrassed and angry because we have a crazy mother, and trying to figure out how the hell to have a normal life. If he cared so damn much he would've thought before he did something that we would've hated him for." He turned abruptly to face his sister. "Tell me you're not defending him."

"I'm not," she replied. "I'm trying not to let anger get the upper hand here." Years of practice at letting emotion and confusion settle and define themselves before she reacted had gotten her through her father's confession. Now, however, faced with her brother's unbridled anger, she realized something else that she had done all her life.

Instead of letting her own anger have its place, she had always deferred it to Douglas—letting him express what she herself felt; letting him have the right, and the freedom, and the relief. And never had she allowed it for herself. Peacemakers never assign guilt, never commit to the wrong cause.

She didn't want to defend him; she wanted to be able to say, without a doubt, that he was wrong, that the secret should never have been kept. But she wondered aloud, "What if Mom had never known, never suspected? What if we would have never known? Wouldn't we be better off?"

"The risk he took was a selfish one," he said. "Unforgivably selfish. He allowed us to blame Mom all these years. He sat back on his precious secret while we all face a lifetime of therapy. No, he can shed a sewer full of tears for all I care—I can't forgive him."

Dhari frowned, at Douglas, at his anger, at her own. He was right, Erin was right, so much needless pain. "I can't forgive him, either; not right now . . . not for a long time."

"Never," he said, dropping his head back against the headrest.

"Don't say never. What he did didn't cause Mom's mental problems, it exacerbated them. And I'm sure he had hoped to avoid that . . . maybe if the drugs, or better therapy, would have helped Mom he wouldn't have cheated at all; or, he might have asked her for forgiveness and gotten it . . . I don't know. I guess I just want to find something good. All I can find is that he must have stayed because he loved her."

"He stayed because of guilt." Douglas stared through the windshield, his hands alternately gripping and releasing the bottom of the steering wheel in the silence. Finally, he asked, "How did she find out?"

"I don't know. With all those years of confusion piled on top of it, we may never know. I'm sure that question has haunted Dad for a long time."

His eyes narrowed and he turned again to face Dhari. "I hope it haunts him for the rest of his life."

"I'm sure it will," Dhari replied. "Even if he is finally forgiven."

Douglas was shaking his head. "Oh, maybe from Donna Too Good—the church requires it . . . do you honestly think Mom will ever be at a place in her head where she'll be able to forgive him?"

"Honestly," she said after a moment, "no . . . maybe after years of therapy, maybe on her deathbed. We can only hope."

"I'll reserve my hope for something more deserving of it."

"What's the alternative, Doug? Hang onto the anger so that none of us can heal?" She thought about the impossibility of it, of how little she really knew about forgiveness. "Some day," she said, "we're going to have to figure out how to forgive."

"Right now I'm just struggling with how to be cordial—for Mom's sake."

"Yeah," Dhari agreed, as the loaner car pulled into view. "We'll start there."

Chapter 29

Usual was not a word Erin could use to describe her life anymore. The day after Dhari left, she had mistakenly assumed that her life would resume as usual. It hadn't. Not only was her personal life filled with thoughts of what she wished could have been with Dhari, but she noticed that her professional life had an added twist as well. The Civil War had become much more personal. In every lecture she saw Nessie's family and Addy and Billy, and wondered how the events of the war might have affected them. The faces of the war were no longer photographs, they were so real that at times she was sure that she could hear them and even smell them. Young boys whooping their ear-piercing war cry, running and sweating, and smelling of gunpowder and warm perspiration. Women, lifting their voices in prayerful song, separating grain from horse manure, and smelling of the earth. The stories from Nessie, the letters and the diaries—and Dhari—had changed her life forever.

But along with these heightened senses came an elevated sense of sadness. She awoke this morning with the thought that she would see Dhari today. Sadly, she remembered that the best she could hope for was a phone call. And even a phone call, she reminded herself, should have purpose. Finally, near the end of the day, and another reading of the diary, she had something purposeful enough, something exciting enough, to justify a call.

"How have you been?" Erin began.

"It's a long story," Dhari replied. "Things didn't go well at the end of Mom's birthday, and the short of it is that she was in an accident. No one else was hurt seriously, but it has caused us all to do some soul searching."

"Oh, I'm sorry, Dhari. I wish you would have called me."

"Everything has been so hectic, and I mean everything. Actually, Mom being in the hospital has been somewhat of a relief; she's at least getting psychiatric care now. It's so different now—new drugs, new ways of looking at mental illness. She never did fit into any one of the old classifications. I read and read and she never did fit. Symptoms of manic-depression and symptoms of compulsion. No wonder the medications messed her up so much."

"Now it's bi-polar and O.C. and a whole new attitude toward individualized treatment. It is a kind of blessing then, for her and for your family."

"I never thought that I'd consider the totaling of my RAV as a blessing," Dhari replied, "but that's the way it's turned out. She came home yesterday, and Dad is taking good care of her."

"I'm sorry that it's been so stressful, Dhari. I wish I could have been of some help for you."

"I've often thought of all of you down there, even with all that's been going on here. Is everyone okay? Have you seen Nessie?"

Erin smiled to herself before answering. "Everyone is fine. I've visited Nessie a few times, and I've called her often. You know, I promised that I'd call you if I found anything interesting in the diaries. I had to know what Nessie had to say, though, before I called you."

There was a noticeable lift in Dhari's voice. "And?"

"And—I want to read you something . . . it's a passage in the earlier diary that caught my attention. Addy's been talking about her pregnancy and the Captain, and how grateful she is to have her mother there for her. Then this: 'I wonder if mother knew my Billy as I do if she would understand the love I feel? If only I could tell her of the tenderness, the exquisite tenderness. How could she deny me that blessing, even now when I am about to embark on motherhood? Would she not want this new life to be nurtured in a love not possible from the Captain? If only I could trust that our secret would be safe, I would tell her of a love like no other. Oh, how I love my Billy, my sweet and tender Billy.'"

There was silence from the other end, so Erin continued. "I've been studying the letters and the diaries, reading them every night, and I kept getting the feeling that there was even more to the secret. Suddenly, it occurred to me."

"God, Erin, as if adultery and murder isn't enough. But don't test my perceptiveness here—tell me."

"Billy was a woman."

Another silence as Erin waited. "You were that sure," Dhari asked, "that you asked Nessie about it?"

"I didn't ask her straight out, not at first. I asked her if there was more about Billy that we didn't know, and I explained how Addy's writings told how he would hold her and soothe her when she was sick or distraught; a quality more commonly attributed to a woman."

"What did she say?"

"Let me see if I can quote her. 'Dat's one a dem tings dat don't need to be talked about 'til it needs to be talked about.'"

Dhari laughed. "You've either been spending way too much time with Nessie, or you've lost your top teeth."

"It's not possible to spend too much time with Nessie," Erin replied.

"So it's true? Billy was a woman?"

"Even as much as I know about women soldiers in the Civil War, it still surprised me."

"Wow, this is going to take some processing ... do you think maybe my grandmother somehow knew that part of the secret? If she even sensed that Addy had felt that kind of love for a woman it would explain why she never accepted her taking her mother's place."

"And it would have added to her justification to separate herself from that part of the family."

"If that truly was why we never knew Anna then society's thinking really has come a long way." Dhari added. "I doubt if today that would be a secret we'd find necessary to keep for a hundred years. I wonder if we will ever know just what she did know."

"Well, my bet is that whatever Anna knew about the situation Nessie also knows. I get the feeling that there wasn't much they kept from each other. And if you don't mind, I'm going to let Nessie tell me everything she wants to. Besides, that'll give me legitimate reasons to call you."

"Friendship is the only reason you need, Erin. And I have to admit having a lesbian saga right in my own family is making me very curious."

Erin chuckled. "I'll send the diaries up to you as soon as I read them through once more. Even though I've read them so many times I could recite them from memory, I want to read them this time with a whole different picture in mind. At least with what we know now I'd say that you inherited all the right genes. Maybe that'll help you stop worrying about inheriting your mother's problems."

"Actually, I haven't had enough time to worry about it lately. Maybe it's better that way; I'd slip over and never know it. Poor Douglas would just have to deal with me."

Erin's voice turned serious. "Are you so sure that Jamie wouldn't be there for better or worse, in sickness and in health?"

"I'm sure. She wouldn't allow her family to abuse her; she certainly isn't going to allow me to. But that's about the only thing I am sure of. Things I want and things I need may not be possible without hurting others."

"I'm speaking as a friend now," Erin said. "And this is as unpretentious as I can make it. I think what you have to do is get sure about what you need and the rest of us will just have to be okay with that . . . whatever it is."

Chapter 30

That conversation from weeks ago still bounced around in her head as Erin mechanically made the trip home from work.

Will I really be okay with it, whatever Dhari needs in her life? I said I would. I said I would be okay with a friendship, even a long distance one, with no hope of it ever being anything else. Is that possible? Is it healthy? How long will I hold out futile hope before what I need in my life becomes paramount?

The questions were unsettling, and since she had no answers there was nothing left to do but to return to her life as usual as quickly as possible. And she had worked on doing just that for weeks now. She had filled her days with the challenges of fresh new lectures and made it a point to catch up with colleagues at lunches. Evenings gradually returned to a more normal routine—time for reading and cooking dinner and laundry. Jake got back his restaurant night and Sunday morning brunch with her, and Terri and Joyce provided the occasional evening of friendship. Eventually it will all fall back into place.

And tonight she had promised herself some much needed comfort time. There would be no reading of diaries, Dhari had them now, and no studying or preparing a lecture. Tonight would be filled with ballgames and memories and kettle-corn with Jake.

"Hey, Dad?" she called, dropping her briefcase and keys in their usual spot. "Who's playing tonight?"

"Dad?" she called again when she heard no reply. "Where are you?" He's home; his car is in the drive. Okay, the deck. The glass door was ajar and barks from Pip confirmed that they were there.

Just through the doorway, Erin tripped and nearly fell over pieces of firewood lying on the floor of the deck. Jake was sitting in one of the chairs with Pip holding her station on his lap. She continued to bark as Erin approached.

Erin's concern was immediate. Jake's face was ashen, his eyes staring and unfocused. "Dad!" she said, rushing to him in a state of panic. She touched his face; his skin was cool and covered with perspiration. "Dad," she repeated as she knelt beside him and took his hand. "How long have you been sitting here?"

His eyes moved slowly to focus on her face; his lips parted as if he would speak but no words formed.

Erin rushed into the house and returned in seconds with her cell phone. She dialed 911 and wiped the dampness from Jake's brow with her hand. As calmly as she could she gave her address and Jake's symptoms and stayed on the open line.

"Dad, do you have pain anywhere?"

He looked again as if he would speak, but did not.

"He's conscious," Erin told the operator, "but he isn't responding. "Okay . . . yes . . . what can I do while we wait?"

She held his hand and continued speaking calmly. "Yes, he's sitting comfortably . . . okay . . . yes, that's two blocks away . . . I hear the siren. Thank you . . . I'll stay on the line until then."

Within minutes the ambulance arrived. Erin rushed through the house and directed the paramedics to the deck. She picked up Pip, who was reluctant to leave Jake's lap, and watched as the men went to work.

Quickly, they checked his eyes and his vital signs. "What is his name?" one paramedic asked.

"Jake," she replied. "His name is Jake." She took a deep breath and resisted asking what they think is wrong. 'Don't panic him' the operator had told her. 'Keep him calm.'

"Jake?" the other medic said. "We're going to lift you onto this giant skateboard here, and give you a ride in our fancy rig out there."

"Are you his daughter?" He nodded at Erin's reply and added, "Contact his doctor and have him meet you at the hospital."

They settled Jake on the stretcher, and Erin took his hand again. "I'm going to get the doctor's number and put Pip in the bedroom, then I'll ride right along with you."

She watched Jake all the way to the hospital, watched his breathing, watched everything the medic did. She was vigilant and more frightened than she had ever been in her life. But, then something happened that took Erin completely by surprise—she became angry.

She gripped her father's hand tightly while the anger gathered and steeped and threatened containment. Damn you, Jake. Damn you! She bowed her head and struggled back the tears. Don't you dare do this. Don't you dare leave me now. Not now—not alone like this. You're all I have, Jake Hughes; you're all I have.

She could no longer stop them, tears dropped heavily on the edge of the stretcher. Tears for whom? For him? Or tears for me? Selfish woman, how can you cry for yourself while the man who raised you, who loves you, is struggling for his life?

"Don't leave me," she whispered, tear-blurred eyes watching shallow breaths fog the oxygen mask. "Please don't leave me."

The intensity of lights and siren gave way to the wait of hospital procedure, while fear and self-admonishment filled Erin's conscious thoughts. She filled out forms and paced and waited and filled out more forms. Hours later, Dr. Bracken finally provided some information to ease her mind.

"He's stable, Erin," he said, "and looking much better than when you brought him in here."

Erin closed her eyes and took a deep breath. "Thank you, Doctor."

"I've scheduled some tests, and I'll go over what they involve with you tomorrow. At this point we need to identify the extent of the blockage in the vessels to his heart. Then we'll be able to plot out a course of action." He put his hand on Erin's shoulder. "But you've both been through enough today. Go on in now; he's anxious to see you."

Erin entered the room, relieved and pleased at what she saw. Jake was propped up in bed, alert and sipping water through a straw. His cheeks pinked and he smiled when he saw her. She leaned over the bed and kissed him and hugged him hard. "I love you," she said against his ear.

"I know, Angel. I see it in your face everyday," he replied. "I'm sorry I scared you like that."

She nodded and forced a smile.

"Sit down here, now," he said. "We have to talk."

Erin pulled the chair close to the bed and took his hand.

"I don't know why it takes something like this to make a person sit up and take stock. You would have thought I would have done this when we lost your mother. My own mother used to tell me I was a cabbagehead. She was right." His voice took on a seriousness Erin hadn't heard for some time. "I nearly lost my chance to ask your forgiveness."

Erin frowned. "Forgiveness for what, Dad?"

"For not telling you something I should have told you a long time ago . . . at least I should have told you after your mother was gone."

"You do know something about my biological parents."

He shook his head. "Not much. And certainly not enough to get your hopes up, or so I thought. But, you know, Honey, that shouldn't have been my call. I know that now. It should have been yours to do with what you wanted all along. I hope you can forgive me for that."

"I already have," she said. "For years I've known that you were protecting Mom. I only wish I could have proven to her that no matter what I found, it would never have changed my love for her."

"Get my wallet out of the drawer there," he said, pointing to the white metal stand beside the bed.

She retrieved it and handed to him, surprisingly less anxious than she had imagined.

He pulled something from an inside compartment and handed it to Erin. It was a clothing tag with the name Phillips written in ink.

"Is this me?" Erin asked.

"I don't know. That's why I hesitated to even give it to you. It was on one of the little shirts in your bag. But, it could've belonged to another and gotten mixed up, or it could even have been a shirt from a charity or secondhand store. Your mother thought it was a boy's name without the apostrophe . . . I just couldn't throw it away."

Erin held the little piece of fabric as if it were a lost piece of the Dead Sea Scrolls. She said the name almost reverently. "Phillips." It didn't matter what name it was, or what the improbabilities. Her only thought was that she wanted it to be hers.

"It may be nothing, Honey," he said. "And if it is, please forgive this old man for giving you false hope."

"There is nothing to forgive, there never will be."

Chapter 31

The phone call from Terri was expected, the survey had been done, but the additional news she offered was not. Jake was in the hospital. It was all Dhari needed to know. Four hours later, she was in the first standby seat available on a plane for Atlanta.

A few phone calls from the airport for a status check and directions, and she was on her way to the hospital. There had been little time for thought, and even now, concern had to be expressed in spurts between reading directions and watching for signs.

When it rains it pours. Tragedies come in threes. Why can't clichés be full of shit? At least the ones with such devastating possibilities. After number two all you can think of is what could be next. More angst, more worry. Exactly why I shouldn't believe in clichés. There will not be a number three. I don't even want to think about a number three.

She spotted the hospital sign on the left, waited for her chance to switch lanes, and squeezed in. He'll be okay, he will. He's younger than Nessie—My God, it could have so easily been Nessie! She could have been gone so quickly. I never would have had the chance to tell her that I loved her. Or Dad. What if it had been Dad? What if I never had the chance to tell him that I know I have no right to judge him—that I promise not to judge him? I need to do better here Dad, I promise to do better.

Dhari concentrated on the signs, wheeled the rental car around the turns toward the parking lot and found a space. As she hurried through the automatic doors her first thought was of Erin. She's so alone, she has no one else. I've got to let her know that I'm here.

A wrong turn took her the long way to the elevator, but she finally stepped into the third floor hallway and spotted Erin waiting at the nurse's station.

"How is he?" she asked, rushing the last few steps and grabbing Erin in an embrace. "How are you?"

Erin held the embrace long and tight. "A whole lot better than yesterday," she said quietly. "Both of us." She cleared her throat as she released Dhari, and took a deep breath. "Come on, he knows you're coming."

Dhari's voice was light and fresh. "Hey, Jake," she said, breezing into his room. "This is not acceptable, you know. There is no way this is going to get you out of that fishing date you promised me."

Jake's cheeks gained color as a smile widened across his face. He held out his hand and she slipped hers into the thick warm grip. "Just a sympathy ploy," he said with a squeeze of her hand, "to get you to come see me."

"Okay, so it worked. Now when are you checking out of this luxury hotel?"

"Ask the boss here," he said, rolling his head to face Erin.

"They're going to do angioplasty to the vessel where they found the most blockage," explained Erin. "The surgery is scheduled for the day after tomorrow. If all goes well, he'll be home by the end of the week."

Dhari sounded relieved. "Oh, that's good news—very good news."

"Erin told me about your mother. That you still came down means a lot to this old man."

"I know it does," Dhari replied. "Is there anything else I can do to brighten up your day?"

Jake found the button and raised the head of the bed a little. "There, now I can see those pretty brown eyes better." He grunted as he pushed himself up against the pillows. "You know the best thing you could do for me is to take my Angel here somewhere and get her talking about something other than me."

"I think I can do that," Dhari said with a smile.

Erin pulled a folded blanket on top of the sheet over Jake's feet. "Are you sure there's nothing else I can get you?"

"Not a thing," he said with a shake of his head.

But Erin continued fussing. She placed the nurse's button on top of the sheet in clear sight, turned on the television and put the remote on the tray next to the bed, and filled his water glass.

Jake squeezed Dhari's hand and released it. "Help me out here," he said. "I'm a fish drowning in sweet potato sauce."

Dhari sent him a wink and started for the door. "Come on, Erin, he's trying to be polite about missing the game."

"Okay," Erin relented. "Remember that Betsy has insisted on staying with you tonight . . . The phone is right here, my cell phone number is taped right on it. The nurses have it at the station taped on the desk. If you feel bad at all, you call me."

"With Betsy here and the nurses in here flirting with me every fifteen minutes," he replied. "I won't have time to feel bad."

Erin pointed her finger at him. "I mean it," she said, joining Dhari at the door.

"I love you, Angel," he said. "I'll see you tomorrow."

"See?" Dhari said, as Pip strutted in the front door and down the hall of the Grayson house, "there's nothing to worry about, Betsy's got tonight covered."

Erin offered no objection. Overnight bag in hand, she followed Dhari down the hall. "She's either the best neighbor in the world, or she has a little twinkle going for Jake."

"Twinkle or not, she'll be watching over Jake, and you can relax. It's getting late. Let's get settled upstairs and then maybe you could read me some more of the diaries. I haven't even taken them out of my backpack yet." Dhari stopped at the doorway to the sitting room and turned on the light. She looked quickly around the room, then shut off the light.

"Is something wrong?" Erin asked.

"No. Just checking to see if Nessie has been here. That rocker by the window? I always move it into the room by the table, and the next day it's right back there at the window. It's either a little game she plays, or a habit. I couldn't bring myself to ask her. I figure she has as much of a right to be in this house as I do, maybe more. I didn't want her to think otherwise. Either way, though, I know she's been here." I hope to God that she's been here. I'm not even going to think about the alternative. "Come on, Pip's already made her downstairs check and is headed up."

The handheld showerhead in the old bathtub was remarkably efficient, so it didn't take long for the women to shower and get settled. Dhari took a deep breath of cool air as she left the steamy bathroom. How is it possible to feel so relaxed, so comfortable in the midst of all this upheaval? Shouldn't the stress be eating away at my stomach lining by now? Have I ever felt this kind of calm? It's joy, she decided, pure and simple. Joy to be in this house, creaky floors and all. Joy to hold Pip in my arms and kiss her little face. Joy to look into Erin's eyes. Is this how life decisions are made—they happen? Like sorting coins in a counter, they bounce around until they settle neatly into the only place they fit? And all the angst and worry about making the right choices just come down to knowing that it's right when it happens? If only I had known not to fight the very things that would bring me joy.

The sight as she entered Addy's room, however, dropped joy quickly from her thoughts. Erin was sitting on the bed, knees drawn up, Pip licking the tears from her face before they could fall.

"Erin?" Dhari moved to the bed as Erin wiped her face, and

sat down next to her. "He's going to be all right."

Erin turned her face away and Dhari reached over to gently pull it back. "He is, Erin."

"For now," she replied, redness beginning to surround the blue of her eyes. "But someday he won't be."

Dhari slipped her arm around Erin's shoulders and pulled her close. "We all have to face that someday, but not today. We don't have to deal with the inevitable today."

"But I wasn't prepared for the anger, Dhari. I have never in my life felt such anger. I cursed him—my father, the person I love most in this world—and I cursed him." Tears began filling her eyes again. "He could have died and all I could think of was how dare he leave me alone, how dare he take the secret with him."

"The secret of who your parents are?"

Erin nodded against the side of Dhari's head. "Suddenly I was sure that he knew, and I was terrified that he wasn't going to tell me—it was so real—the loneliness was so real." She lifted her head, her face so close, her eyes so affecting. "He gave me a name, and it could be mine, but it still feels like the earth has dropped out from beneath me—that horrible feeling of panic that wakes you in the middle of the night when there is no one there to hold you, no one to take away the panic. It frightens me to think that when he's gone that feeling will be with me forever."

"No, Erin, it won't." Dhari took Erin's face in her hands. "It won't. I won't let it." She touched Erin's lips tenderly with her own, felt them quiver and soften. She left them for a moment to whisper, "I won't leave you."

Erin met Dhari's eyes with apparent understanding. "I need to believe you," she said softly. "I need to right now."

"You can," Dhari whispered, then kissed Erin again. She touched her lips lightly, so very lightly, moved like a whisper over down-soft cheeks, held like a warm breath over delicate eyelids. She was showing Erin so slowly, so carefully, what she had never felt before. What came from deep inside her, welling from a depth unknown. Love, I'm showing you love.

Erin moved closer, wrapping her arms around Dhari's waist. She brought her mouth to Dhari's, firmer now, her lips parting in submission. And Dhari entered, tentatively exploring the warmth. Twinges of excitement shot through her chest, but still she moved slowly. She would account for every second, once again savor every minute.

Erin's head dropped gently back as moist lips traveled the length of her neck. The words were breathed against her throat, "You fill my heart, Erin."

Her voice was low and soft as she pulled Dhari with her to lie back against the pillows. "I hope I always will."

Dhari gazed into the eyes she had committed to memory. They were telling her of love, of how special she was, while Erin's hands slipped beneath the loose T-shirt and slid up the length of Dhari's back. She lowered herself into Erin's embrace. Supple breasts, clad in thin fabric, pressed against her own. Bare legs slid around the smoothness of her thigh. A lover's embrace—full and sensuous—beginning the melt toward passion.

Open and wet, their lips met now in a deepening kiss. The give and take of it gathered sensations deep within Dhari; a sigh of pleasure sent them shooting through her body.

Heat penetrated the fabric that kept flesh from flesh. Everywhere Dhari's hands touched there was heat—along Erin's side, over her hip, down the bareness of her thigh—everywhere their bodies touched she felt it. Dhari thought no more of futures or risks; her singleness of mind was to lay her hand over Erin's breast, to claim her right to linger there.

With the tip of her tongue Dhari traced the fullness of Erin's mouth in a promise to return, and sent a shiver through Erin's body with a path to her ear. "I want to take away the loneliness," she breathed, as her hand found its way under Erin's shirt and moved with deliberate slowness over the contours and planes. A quiver as she covered the plane of her abdomen, a sudden breath as her caress rounded over Erin's chest. "I want to love you."

Dhari pressed her lips to the hollow of Erin's throat, and was met with a moan of deepening pleasure. She drew her hand lightly over the path to Erin's abdomen where her fingers lifted and ran their tips along the elastic waistband. Erin's hips shifted in response and she breathed the words almost imperceptibly, "I love how you make me feel…yes," she whispered as Dhari's hand covered her breast and teased the hardening nipples. "You make me so happy."

Quickly Erin lifted Dhari's shirt over her head and then shed her own. "I need to feel you against me," Erin said. "Your hands, your breasts, your mouth…all of you."

And Dhari complied, letting her hands learn the beauty of Erin's body; running them over the flushed flesh of her chest and the round softness of her breasts, to the hollows that trembled with desire. She stripped away the last of Erin's clothing, letting her hands feel the magic of arousal beneath them. The deepness of Erin's breathing brought her breast to Dhari's lips. As ardently as her hands had sought the very essence of Erin, so did Dhari's mouth. Revisiting, tantalizing all the right places—lingering there until Erin's hands clutched the sheet, her breath trembling with excitement. Only then did Dhari slip between Erin's legs, lifting and kissing the length of tender flesh high inside her thighs. Erin's hands let go of the sheet to grasp Dhari's head. Her body arched and with a gasp she pulled Dhari's mouth to her.

Slowly Dhari stroked, feeling the exquisite silk ripple under her tongue. Slowly through the wetness, stroking, stroking, searching the swollen folds, tasting the salty crevices. Long and slowly she explored, moving her lips and her tongue to press tenderly here, harder there. Erin's cries of pleasure filled the stillness of the room, and the rhythm began—a measuring of movement that Dhari matched with the pressure of her mouth.

She resisted the urge to hurry, to rush Erin to that frenzied state of ecstasy. She deftly slipped her hands beneath Erin's hips and lifted them, responding to the rhythm that moved the sweet wetness against her mouth. Taking command of her, the rhythm grew in intensity until it throbbed throughout her own body. Dhari was dizzy with the scent of her, close to coming simply from the feel of trembling thighs and the sounds of desire. Never had she rejoiced in giving such pleasure; never had it mattered this much.

Erin's fingers, laced in Dhari's hair, suddenly stopped in their grasp. Her hips, too, halted their rhythm. Dhari closed her lips around the tiny hard center. A shudder shook Erin's body, and her hips pressed fiercely upward. She was coming, coming to Dhari, needing Dhari, enslaving Dhari with the thrill of her need.

Erin cried out, a long exalting cry escaping her arched body as it held itself for a moment suspended in ecstasy. And Dhari answered her with her own cry, "It's you, Erin. It is you I love."

Dhari wrapped her arms around Erin and held her until Erin slipped down, exhausted, into the folds of the bed and her heartbeat, pounding in Dhari's ear, returned to normal.

How do you measure love? By a count of kisses? By the heat of its fire, or the length and intensity of its passion? Maybe it can't be measured.

"Do I have the right to love you?" Erin asked softly. "Because I do; I do love you, Dhari."

"Yes, oh, yes," Dhari said, laying kisses over Erin's glistening skin. "This is where I belong. This is where I'll stay."

She snuggled into the pleasant curve of Erin's body, content to watch her own hand tracing an imaginary line over creamy soft breasts. She drew a long, deep breath as the cadence of her own heartbeat began to slow, expecting Erin to drift into sleep.

At length, they lay comfortably in each other's arms. Pip, welcomed at last from the end of the bed, had curled herself into the curve of Dhari's stomach. There were more gentle caresses and tender kisses. The words that took form in Dhari's mind at this moment were those of Elizabeth Barrett Browning, tumbling uncalled into consciousness. She had always thought the poem overly sentimental, irrelevant to her life, but now it spoke the meaning she had missed. She lifted her face and whispered into Erin's hair, "I love thee to the level of every day's most quiet need—"

"By sun and candlelight," Erin finished, her lips lightly brushing Dhari's temple. "It's what I've hoped for most in my life . . . an unconditional and simple love, a love that sustains. I never thought . . . " She stopped mid-sentence and reached across to the table next to the bed. She picked up the little clothing tag and stared hard at the name. "I always thought it could come only from my family." She kissed the side of Dhari's face. "Now, have I found it in you?"

Dhari answered reflectively. "I would never have thought so before today." She took the fabric gently from Erin's fingers. "Phillips?" she said after a moment. "Is this the name Jake gave you?"

The gentle beginning of a smile gave Erin a look of resolve. "When I first saw it, it didn't even register that it was Billy's last name, or matter that it could just be a little boy's name on a T-shirt. It's such a common name, first and last, and all I could think of was that maybe it is possible that it could be my name too. But realistically," she said, looking directly into Dhari's eyes, "the improbability is pretty high. I know that."

"I promise, if this is you," Dhari said into the shining blueness, "we're going to find it out together."

The night was black; the only light was that of a half moon reflecting off the pale boards of the house. Nessie rose from the wooden bench, set the Billy doll in her place, and emerged from the canopy of the old tree.

Mooned highlights shone in the coal black of her eyes as she peered through the darkness at the sitting room window. "Leave outta dat chair now, Anna," she said, pulling an old photograph from the pocket of her dress and passed her fingertips over the faded image. "She's home, now. Won't be no more need for window-watchin'."